follow me too

a handbook
of movement activities
for three- to five-year-olds

by Marianne Torbert, Ph.D. and Lynne B. Schneider, M.A.
of The Leonard Gordon Institute for Human Development Through Play
of Temple University, Philadelphia, Pennsylvania

Addison-Wesley Publishing Company
Menlo Park, California • Reading, Massachusetts • New York
Don Mills, Ontario • Wokingham, England • Amsterdam • Bonn
Sydney • Singapore • Tokyo • Madrid • San Juan • Paris
Seoul, Korea • Milan • Mexico City • Taipei, Taiwan

To Raymond, who taught his little sister to play, and in so doing opened her life to a very special joy and celebration that only a few are privileged to experience.

—Marianne

With love and gratitude to my parents, Doris and Enar Bredberg, my grandmother, Maude Frost, and my aunt, Florence Bennette, who gave me much to follow; and to my children, Nancy and Michael Schneider, whose love and joy follow me too.

—Lynne

The games in this book are reorganized and revised from *Follow Me: A Handbook of Movement Activities for Children* (1980) with copyright permission.

Managing Editor: Diane G. Silver
Senior Editor: Lois Fowkes
Production Manager: Janet Yearian
Production Coordinator: Barbara Atmore
Design Manager: Jeff Kelly
Text Design: Michelle Taverniti
Cover Design: Rachel Gage
Illustrations: Rachel Gage

Jell-O is a registered trademark of Kraft General Foods, Inc.

ISBN 0-201-81597-4
 2 3 4 5 6 7 8 9 10 - AL - 95 94 93

About the authors

One author spent part of her childhood in an apartment in Newark, New Jersey, one in the streets of East Cleveland, Ohio.

One found no pleasure in games as a child; one found all the joy and celebration of play.

One is an elementary teacher; one is a college professor.

Marianne Torbert and Lynne Schneider make a wonderful team that is sensitive and caring about the benefits and traumas of childhood play. They are the director and assistant director of the Leonard Gordon Institute for the Development Through Play of Temple University.

Marianne and Lynne wrote this book to share with you and your children the joy and growth that is available in carefully selected and recreated games and activities. Through the games presented here the authors hope that you will reap the rewards of enhancing the quality of children's lives as you help them reach toward competency. They wish for you the joy that accompanies this venture.

Acknowledgments

A special thanks to Lois Klevan and Sherry McBride, practitioners who have gone the extra mile to make this a better book. And thanks to the Philadelphia School District Head Start Program Director, Rosemary D. Mazzatenta, the Early Childhood Field Coordinator, Linda Notto Stulz, and the leadership class of 1991-1992: Maxine H. Darden, Marilyn W. Khan, Geneva Szatny, Mary Ellen Hence, Sue Carol Dudley, Kathleen Miller Dzura, Ursula Shockley-Rice, Sherita Thompson Daniels, Glorious D. Bright, Judith E. Major, Vickie Cliett-Hill, Catherine M. Link, Anice L. Dickerson-Watters, Bernice Lowery-Johnson, Elizabeth Woodson, June F. Dorsey, and Barbara Monley.

What reviewers have said about
Follow Me Too

"*Follow Me Too* gives you over fifty games and activities that are selected to help children build important life skills while having fun. Having spent many years observing and supervising teachers of preschoolers, I only wish that I could have made such a book available to them.

If you teach or are a parent of a three- to five-year-old, you need *Follow Me Too* on your reading list and never too far from your immediate reach."

Marie Morrison
Early Childhood Specialist
Wellfleet, Massachusetts

"I have just completed my review of your book *Follow Me Too* and found it to be a delightful handbook for early childhood educators who are interested in expanding the movement experiences they present to their children. I was impressed with the fact that most of the activities in the book were presented in such a way that a creative teacher could easily expand upon each idea. Yet at the same time, the activities are presented clearly enough so that a young and inexperienced teacher can implement them without any diffficulty."

Susan D.G. Warford
Child Development Center
University of Rhode Island

"I have used your *Follow Me Too* handbook since a fall workshop for DAEYC. It is wonderful. I love it, my children love it, and my two student teachers love it."

Sandi Dahn
Kindergarten Teacher
Wilmington, Delaware

Contents

preface

The role of play in planning for tomorrow

Living effectively in today's world requires personal effort and self-determination, and our children will face even greater complexity. Anthropologists believe that the next steps in human development will involve increased use of the incredible potential we already possess. We have been told that we now use only 10 percent of the potential available within our human capacity. How can we unlock the other 90 percent? We feel that play may awaken some of that dormant potential.

Children's play takes many forms. Some of these forms of play are free play; sociodramatic play; solitary play; board games; and active, organized, group games and activities. While each of these is valuable and can be incorporated into developmentally focused programs, *Follow Me Too: A Handbook of Movement Activities for Three- to Five-Year-Olds* is concerned with active, organized, group games and activities. These games and activities are carefully selected to allow children to develop important social, emotional, physical, and cognitive skills that create the foundation upon which growth can most successfully take place.

We are beginning to become more sensitive to the basics that underlie the traditional basics of reading, writing, and arithmetic. We have begun to look carefully at what is truly basic to the ability to learn. Underlying the processes of input, processing, utilization, and retention are very relevant foundation skills. For example, children who have never learned to focus and pay attention will have difficulty consistently processing input and developing the sense of familiarity that allows for pattern recognition. Children who have gained these skills experience success, which produces feelings of competency and positive self-regard. The curiosity that encourages participation and further exploration is kindled, and actually motivates greater efforts in focusing and paying attention.

Evidence of the contribution that one skill makes to the growth of other skills is seen throughout the learning process. A few of the interactive (reciprocal) skills involved are focusing; paying attention; concentrating and perceiving, including listening and taking clues from one's environment; generating alternatives and making decisions; persevering; practicing self-determination; learning appropriate social interaction skills; using memory; and handling, dealing with, and releasing stress. In the past, many children gained these skills by chance rather than by design. The children who gained these skills were successful in school, and those who did not experienced failure.

Dr. John Lawther, child development expert, explains that feelings and learning tend to build upon earlier experience. Growth and development actually owe their efficiency to the slow and inefficient learning that has gone before. Practitioners have found that selecting specific games to meet specific developmental needs of their children (developing attention span, concentration, listening skills, self-control, perseverance, and so on) and using such games on a consistent basis contribute to children's growth in these specific skills.

Active, organized games, carefully selected and well planned, can become a pleasurable means (tool) by which children can build a strong sense of accomplishment while they gain many of the foundation skills that will allow them to deal more effectively with an increasingly complex and stressful world. We believe that the games in this book create an environment for such skills to develop naturally.

If a game qualifies in relation to the development of one or more relevant social, emotional, cognitive, and/or physical skills, it should also be constructed or reconstructed to include every child with sufficient opportunities ("expansion") and give each player means or choices that allow him or her to enter and participate at an individual growth level. This concept is known as *equity* or *equalization.* This type of play allows no room for subtle or blatant elimination of any child. Perfection is not the goal. Growth for *every* child (which can seem erratic) and an accompanying sense of competency are the objectives.

Dr. Robert White, a Harvard professor famous for his classic study "Motivation Reconsidered" (1959) explains the vital role of play:

> *Play may be fun, but it is also a serious business in childhood. During these hours the child steadily builds up her/his competence in dealing with the environment.*

The major goal of the Leonard Gordon Institute for Human Development Through Play of Temple University is to select, modify, create, and disseminate movement activities that will meet children's social, emotional, mental, and physical needs. To accomplish this, play and game environments must be planned to allow every child to enter each activity without threat or boredom and be challenged at a personal level. The child can then celebrate growing and contribute to the growth of others. Such an environment supports and encourages trust, autonomy, initiative, and bonding of participants. The Institute continually studies the needs of children and analyzes activities and games to determine how better to meet them.

The games found in *Follow Me Too: A Handbook of Movement Activities for Three- to Five-Year-Olds* do not constitute a curriculum or even a program. Instead, they are tools to be used in reaching the objectives of developmentally appropriate programs for preschool-age children. These games/activities have been developed over a long period of time and continue to be field tested by practitioners like yourself, who in turn make suggestions and indicate problems or limitations. We at the Leonard Gordon Institute for Human Development Through Play of Temple University then reassess and attempt to incorporate suggestions and improvements to meet the expressed needs and recommendations. We hope you will find that the efforts of many have made the games within this book positive and pleasurable tools that can help your children grow, develop, and learn in an environment that is physically, socially, and emotionally safe and filled with joy and celebration.

Marianne Torbert
Lynne B. Schneider

introduction

Play may be the key to unlock many doors.

This book has been written and designed to give you practical and easy games to play in small spaces, indoors or outdoors, rain or shine, any time during the day, for long or short periods of time. These games can be used for transition activities, to calm children down, for class management, and for growth. A life skills list at the beginning of each game allows you to see the game's value at a glance. Suggestions and modifications help you tailor each game to meet the needs of your children.

Developmental skills such as focusing, paying attention, being a good listener, learning from the environment, sharing, trusting, becoming autonomous, taking initiative, persevering, building self-esteem, and moving well can be nurtured within these carefully selected and developed, organized, active games.

Our view of play in relation to participation in organized, active games

Over the years it has been discovered that organized, active games have certain very exciting potentials that come to fruition only when those who direct or affect the experiences view play and players in certain ways. The following parameters[1] have evolved to clarify the appropriate view of play and players:

1. The players are the most important part of any play experience.
2. Players (people) have needs.
3. Play behavior may be an attempt to deal with unmet needs.
4. An individual's view of self, others, and the world can be affected by play experiences.
5. When skillfully planned, movement activities have the potential to meet important developmental needs.
6. Everyone has the right to healthy, positive play experiences. It is our responsibility to find ways to make this type of play available to all.
7. We can continuously become more sensitive to needs and more skillful at selecting, modifying, and creating movement activities to meet these needs.
8. Present play activities need to be studied carefully in relation to both their positive and negative effects upon participants.

[1] Adapted from *Follow Me: A Handbook of Movement Activities for Children.* (Torbert, 1980)

It is hoped that you will find excitement in using organized games as an effective tool, and through experience gain a growing proficiency in the ability to select, modify, and create activities to meet children's needs.

The approach used in this book based upon our view of play

This book will

- Consider *growth and development* needs as basic to planning, selecting, modifying, and creating activities.
- Consider the importance of *positive inclusion* and true mainstreaming through attempting to continuously incorporate *expansion*, *equalization*, *progressive challenges*, and *interactive challenge*.

The following terms and definitions are used throughout this book:

Expansion—increasing the number of turns or opportunities to participate in important developmental experiences and activities.

Equalization—giving each player an opportunity to participate at her or his level of ability.

Progressive challenges—the availability of multiple levels of difficulty (choices) within an activity, so that each individual participant is free to continuously choose a level of challenge, thus building a personal progression of growth.

Interactive challenge—equalization that allows participants, who vary in abilities, to be able to interact and reciprocally contribute to each other's growth process.

The following is an example of how games can be changed to incorporate our approach.

Musical Chairs

The history of play and games has not been fun and frivolity for everyone. If you doubt this, find ten adults and ask them about their childhood play experiences. Our own interviews have turned up sagas of pain and devastation by too many.

Musical Chairs is used as an example because most people know it and because it is an elimination game that has left many five-year-olds in tears, although they were told it would be fun.

Children learn a great deal about life and themselves through play. At the age at which Musical Chairs becomes a popular game, children are beginning to enjoy participating together in a somewhat loosely organized structure. Most adults would like the children to learn to share and gain "appropriate" social skills. Many of these same well-meaning adults then offer Musical Chairs as an opportunity to play with others, without examining this experience.

What is the child learning? "Grabbing a chair for myself is what really pays off, so it's me first, even if I have to knock my new friend out of the way. I don't like being inactive or left out, so I guess this is THE way. It must be the 'best' way, or why else would only the one who can push everyone else out of the way win the only prize?"

And what about the loser? The experience of being eliminated in Musical Chairs can teach children that they are losers. And how is it possible to gain the ability to become a winner if participation is reduced to watching others play?

Consider modifying this game to be a positive experience for all:

- Eliminate elimination.
- Change the focus of the game from "me first" to "we can."

Is it possible to increase the number who walk away from a game feeling good? Does someone have to feel like a loser to allow someone else to feel like a winner? Does this approach make games less fun, less exciting, less vigorous?

4

- Reduce potential for emotional and social as well as physical injury.
- Make everyone a winner.

These changes led to the creation of "Islands," found in the games section of this book. Try it!

Now if you have only one prize, put it in the closet and award all the children the real prize: the joy and celebration of playing and working together to conquer the task (the competition).

The games selected for *Follow Me Too* support and facilitate the first three stages of development according to Erik Erikson.

Trust, autonomy, initiative
(summarized by Marianne Torbert)

Trust

A child who experiences positive nurturing develops basic trust, a sense that "I am going to be taken care of," that things are safe and secure. A child exposed to new situations that have not previously been experienced must continue to build and transfer this trust to the new.

A child that experiences the ability to do things also begins to build a basic self-trust: "I am able. I can."

Factors related to this stage: Repetition of experience allows a child to begin to recognize patterns and consistency, to gain skills, to have an orientation, to establish continuity. From this familiarity, life can begin to be predictable.

The energy conserved by a sense of security, the power of predictability, and an increasing sense of competency allows the child to begin to move toward risking, trying, exploring, learning, developing autonomy.

Autonomy

In becoming more independent, self-governing, self-reliant, and self-determining, a personal and individual identity begins to unfold. The child begins to have a sense of self, finds that there are choices and challenges to be experienced, and may discover that perseverance pays off. This new sense of self (and growing sense of competency) may also manifest itself in testing for personal control, occasional or even frequent refusal to comply, and the discovery of "No!"

Factors related to this stage: Children are given the opportunity to make choices, meet challenges at the individual level, make decisions, discover themselves through interactions with others, and begin to develop self-control and responsibility.

This taking charge of oneself also builds self-confidence and allows one to start to take initiative.

Initiative

The growing individual experiments with different roles, discovering preferences. If one is grounded in basic trust and autonomy, then it becomes safe to assume more responsibility.

Factors related to this stage: Given safe opportunities, children become willing to try something new, solve problems, generate alternatives, make contributions, take risks, and perhaps even take a leadership role.

No stage of development stands by itself, nor can one be cleanly separated from the others. Each makes its contribution to, and is affected by the others. Development in all stages continues throughout life, although certain periods in the developmental process seem to be more focused upon the characteristics of one stage or another. Our task is to support children's growth toward their potential through the development of appropriate experiences and environments.

Movement activities can allow a child to process life in the following ways:

- To read one's environment; to perceive, process, and respond.
- To try out, test, evaluate, and try again.
- To store in order to anticipate later effects and make predictions.
- To begin to work through the events that are occurring in one's life.
- To develop social, emotional, cognitive, and physical skills and coping processes.
- To determine what works and what doesn't work.
- To make discoveries.

Active, organized, carefully planned games can be an effective tool for growth and development. Left to chance, they can also become a source of trauma and self-doubt.

Bela Mittelman (Department of Psychiatry, New York University College of Medicine) has noted both the negative and positive potential of physical experiences in his study of motility. "Inadequate motor performance leading to derogatory comments or rejection by parents or other children may be one of the most significant sources of the feeling of inadequacy,"[1] whereas "adequate solution of the motor problem is attended by joy and leads to repetition."[2]

Why use movement activities?

Play is exciting and fun-filled. Its elusive qualities draw and hold its participants' energies and concentration. There is a virtually inexhaustible supply of movement activities that are flexible and can be modified or progressively changed to meet specific group needs.

[1] Bela Mittelman, "Motility in Infants, Children, and Adults," in *Psychoanalytic Studies of the Child*, 9, 1954, p. 167.
[2] Ibid., p. 174.

Movement activities are action-based and observable. Not only the planner but also the participant is receiving immediate and constant evaluative feedback. Just as one learns muscular control through frequent and repetitive experiences, so may play be a tool to evaluate social interactions and to experience and deal with various emotional responses and personal feelings.

Well-planned play may increase a child's willingness to become involved, and in turn, more ready for the experiences that follow. Activities that allow a child to solve a problem, make a viable decision, or feel personal success seem to increase active efforts to cope and willingness to take chances. This effect certainly goes beyond the historically acknowledged value of play as simply a means of letting off steam or reducing stress.

> *The personal satisfaction that a participant derives from being able to do something well is an important factor in his concept of himself. In other words, motor development as well as mental development is vital from the standpoint of mental health.*[1]

> *Motility (the ability to move well/spontaneously) plays a lifelong significant role in the psychodynamics of every individual, both normal and pathological.*[2]

What is your role?

Those who direct or affect children's play have a vital role in each child's growth and development. The awareness of children's needs, careful selection and perhaps modification of activities, and continuous

---

[1] Arthur Jersild, *Child Psychology.* Englewood Cliffs, N.J.: Prentice-Hall, Inc., 1968, p. 115.
[2] Bela Mittelman, "Motility in Infants, Children, and Adults," in *Psychoanalytic Studies of the Child*, 9, 1954, p. 170.

observation and evaluation can increase the possibility of play experiences being a positive contributor to growth and development.

What are the benefits to the child?

- Good feelings about oneself.
- Increased desire to participate.
- Increased social, emotional, cognitive, and physical skills.

The development of positive growth experiences through well-selected games

Well-selected games have some general characteristics that make them a powerful tool in helping a participant gain a positive view of self (supporting autonomy) and others (supporting group bonding).

Characteristics of well-selected games

- Opportunities to experiment and experience are abundant and continuous; children have lots of safe turns.
- A broad range of differences can be accommodated. Progressive challenges can be built in to allow individuals to participate at their own personal level.
- Effort has been made to reduce potential for emotional and social, as well as physical injury.
- Goals and purposes are clear, consistent, and attainable.
- Feedback is usually immediate and frequent, allowing a participant to experience relationships between cause and effect.
- Errors are expected and forgiven.

- There is usually an almost instant opportunity to try again (to adjust, to repeat, to recover).
- Perseverance and coping with temporary frustration is encouraged by the format of the game.
- Self-control frequently contributes to achieving the goal.
- All of the components of the game tend to enhance the possibility of positive social interactions.
- No player is eliminated either blatantly or subtly.

Some thoughts about preschoolers

(All games mentioned below are found in this book.)

You may want to consider the following ideas when playing games with preschoolers:

1. Preschoolers like the familiar. They enjoy the security of repetition. Knowing what to do allows them to begin to be able to anticipate effects and make predictions, which allows them to increase their sense of trust in the situation and in themselves. This is one reason this age group loves familiar chants and rhymes.

2. You do need to be in control of the group by getting and maintaining attention. This control can be brought about in several ways:

   - Have the children DO something with you. A "Can You?" activity may help— "Can you reach high to the sky? Can you touch your nose? Can you touch your toes? Can you sit down? Can you rub your tummy? Can you clap your hands? Can you scratch your head? Can you go to sleep? Can you stand up *and* turn around? Can you shrug your shoulders? Can you wiggle all over like Jell-O? Can you hide your eyes? Can you cover your ears? Can you melt into a little tiny puddle and be very, very quiet?"

When you begin activities like this, feel comfortable to start with only a few children and hope that the others will notice and join in. Attempting to get all the young children quiet and ready to start at once can be an almost impossible task for them and very frustrating for you.

"Can You?" requires that the children listen to you (something you want them to do), but doesn't require that you talk too long before they can be active. An activity doesn't have to always be very active, but it must allow for continuous involvement. Children get fidgety when they have to wait. As you observe the different effects of the various "Can You?" challenges, you can see that some things lead almost to the edge of chaos, while others tend to be quieting. You may want to finish this activity with a "Can You?" challenge that leaves the children calmed. Example: "Can you go to sleep?" (See the game "Can You?")

"Follow Me" (follow the actions of the leader) is another excellent activity. Once the children are familiar with this activity, it can be used to get their attention any time. The leader simply does a familiar "Follow Me" gesture while looking at one or more children. This encourages participation; others will join in as they notice children doing "Follow Me" motions. It is a wonderful way to get the group's attention and encourage involvement. (See the game "Follow Me.")

- Have children occasionally SIT to play an activity such as "Birds Fly," "I Am a Balloon," "Old MacDonald Had a Body," or even "Jell-O Jiggle" to maintain or gain some additional control. (If overdone this can become ineffective.)

- A circle can give some unity to the situation. "Weather Walks" might be done by the whole group moving around the room. Don't expect perfection. It's not that important.

- You may find that the anticipation and prediction that come with familiarity through repetition of a structure (game, routine) may even bring additional control to the situation without your having to seek it.

3. Preschoolers like to be active, although their self-control may not be very well developed. Games may really be practice in developing self-control and increasing it over time. Games like "Farmer-Farmer" and "Rise and Shine" are particularly good for developing self-control.

4. You may have to simplify a game or activity that seems too complex for preschoolers.

- Reduce the complexity of the goal or purpose of the game. For example, let simple completion of the act, not the speed with which the act can be completed, be the goal.

- In "Find It," ask, "Can each of you find something that is the color blue?" Wait until all have found something blue. Young children enjoy accomplishing something. They usually feel like a winner in the process. This way everyone can be a winner. Too many times adults introduce the concept of a single winner, believing that this is a motivational factor, when the children are already motivated and just want to have the fun of doing. Watch a child play with a balloon. The competition is with the task.

- Break down the activity into parts that can then be added as the children are able to handle a new challenge. In the game "Cows and Ducks," the players are to find all members of their species by listening to the sounds coming from the other players. You could break this down for preschoolers. The children could all make the sound of a cow or a duck. Perhaps you could hold up a picture or drawing and they could respond with the appropriate sound and add actions. You could make the sound of a duck and have all the children respond by going to a designated pond. If you moo like a cow, they all are go to a designated pasture. Build a progression that can be developed over time.

- Slow down the pace of the activity, waiting for all the children to complete the act rather than rushing or racing; even the tone of your voice can make a difference in setting the pace.

- Repeat a simple task several times until the children get the idea. Children enjoy repetition, and they also learn from each other.

- Use the same activity or game over several play periods. (Some children actually put it together between play periods.)

- Reduce the amount of equipment used. For example, there could be too many balloons in "Balloon Keep Up" for a young child to deal with.

- Eliminate competition and encourage cooperation. You might like to attempt to introduce games like "Cross Over," "Help!", "Busy Bee and Back to Back," and "Islands."

- Reduce the amount of group interaction needed to participate. As children grow and experience within groups, they become more able to become involved in activities that require effective group interaction to succeed. As the children mature you might like to attempt to introduce games that encourage helping and sharing.

5. You can learn how to *broaden* the complexity of an activity as the children continue to grow. Expand the variety of choices as each child can handle it rather than simply making the activity more difficult for all. Sometimes an individual child can make an appropriate choice if there are several levels of difficulty to choose from. Begin to look for games that allow for these progressive challenges. Games such as "Farmer-Farmer" allow children to take risks at whatever level they

choose. One can be as creative as one wishes in "Weather Walks" and "I Am a Balloon."

6. Games and activities are developmental in nature.

   - The child.may not show instant or complete success.

   - It is important to observe carefully each child's *changing* response to the activity.

   - Observe children trying new activities and challenges to gain ideas about how you can help them grow.

   - It is important to be patient—real growth is not an instant process, although it may sometimes appear to be.

   - Some activities allow children to put factors within their experience together over time in a *discovery* manner. This is empowering to a child, allowing autonomy (self-determination, self-governance, self-evaluation) to develop. Because it may involve a period of fumbling (discovering), adults can be too empathetic and want to direct the child to the answer(s), thus reducing the opportunity to experience the ability to overcome a difficult challenge. Your task is to engineer the environment so that the child can experience this discovery process.

   - Be careful not to trap yourself into being comfortable only when the activity looks organized or all the children are doing the same thing or doing it the right way.

   - Encourage participation in activities, but allow a child to buy out or respond individually, if she or he is not negatively affecting others.

7. It is important to remember that leaders of games will experience failures as well as successes. We can learn from both. That's what growing from experience is all about.

Play may be the key to unlock many doors!

8. Know why you have selected the activity (goals for growth and development). You can better affect growth and development if you know what's happening within an activity. Movement activities can be a wonderful growth and development tool, or they can be a disaster.

9. Be aware that children have a natural drive to grow.[1] Your job is to make growth opportunities available to the children, not to force them to grow. Unlock doors!

[1] Robert W. White, "Motivation Reconsidered: The Concept of Competence." *Psychological Review*, 66 (5), pages 297-333. Harvard, 1959.

games to get you started

For those of you who would like to get started and would like some suggestions, we are going to recommend two groups of games. The first group of three games—"Follow Me," "Can You?", "Cross Over"—will allow you to get a feel for the games and for your children's responses and reactions.

Give yourself time to read and digest one game at a time. Trying only one new game a day or even a week may allow you to be better prepared and more able to remember just what happened.

Follow Me

Start out with "Follow Me." Read pages 87 and 88, but ignore the Simplifications and Challenges section. Start with a very simple version, and play for only a few minutes the first time. Do not plan to move through all the possible challenges the first day. A real growth-producing game should be absorbed slowly, and like growth, it takes time and repetition.

Attempt to play this game twice the first day. During the second trial, let the game go on a little longer and attempt to observe children as carefully as possible. Later, think about what happened. The next day, start "Follow Me" by simply doing it. You may now have a transition activity that draws the children's attention to you while they are learning

- to focus, attend, and concentrate.
- to read their environment more carefully.
- to increase their ability to note and reproduce specific movements accurately.

The activity also subtly reinforces the wonderful lesson that perseverance can lead to improvement and increased success.

Don't be afraid to repeat the activity several times over several days. If you feel that your children may be getting bored and need a greater challenge, read the Simplifications and Challenges to see if one of them is appropriate.

After children are familiar with the activity, you may find that some want to help you lead "Follow Me." Ask for volunteers. Assist only to the extent that is absolutely necessary. These opportunities help support Erikson's developmental stages of Autonomy and Initiative. Do not push any child into a leadership position, but do make it comfortable for a child to initiate helping you, another child, or the group. Encourage parents or other primary caregivers to ask the child about these games and perhaps play them with the child, allowing each child to try out expressive leadership skills in a safe environment. A parent letter (page 36) can be used to explain steps and objectives.

Can You?

After conquering "Follow Me," "Can You?" may seem comfortable and familiar to the children and to you. "Can You?" is simply the verbal version of "Follow Me." You may want to follow the same pattern of presentation as you did in "Follow Me." Begin with "Follow Me" and slip into adding the question, "Can you...?" Gradually reduce your reinforcing motions and finally give only the verbal challenge.

Don't lose sight of the idea that these games are actually tools for children to learn important life skills. As in "Follow Me," the children practice important growth and development skills:

- Focusing, attending, and concentrating on auditory input
- Decoding the spoken word
- Following verbal instructions
- Persevering
- Accepting a challenge
- Beginning to solve problems

"Follow Me" and "Can You?" are two transitional activities that can be done in whatever space and time is available.

Cross Over

The third suggestion is a game in which children begin to learn to share their limited space with others. Read about "Cross Over." Focusing on the life skills that are being practiced in each of the games will make it possible for us to have a full complement of tools as we help children grow.

Reflections

We hope that you have gained some insight into the value of these games and some little techniques that will help you use these games as a tool to help you do what you do best: assist children in their growth and development process. Always keep in mind that unlike most athletics and sports, these games are not performance oriented. It is not how the activity looks that is so important, but rather what is happening to the players in the process of the activity. Is growth available to each and every child at an individual level? Can children evaluate their own growth? Is each child empowered by this growth and awareness of it? Our focus is not on "practice makes perfect" (which is actually performance oriented), but on planning rich play experiences that can allow the participants to grow in important life skills and can potentially have a positive effect on the rest of each child's life.

A dozen more games to get you started

Wind, Rain, and Thunder
Freeze (This can be started within "Cross Over.")
Busy Bee and Back to Back (This uses skills learned in "Cross Over" and "Freeze.")
Carpet Activities (a real challenge, that builds on the skills of "Cross Over" while allowing more action within less space)
Arrows
Islands
Where Is...?
Bear or Lion Hunt
Jell-O Jiggle
Old MacDonald Had a Body

Sounds to Move By
Find It

Additional related activities are suggested within the game descriptions. As you increase your awareness of these games as a developmental tool, you may want to begin to look through the Life Skills section of the games and select accordingly.

games and suggestions for special needs and situations

Attention-getting activities

We have found that once children are familiar with the following activities, we can get their attention by starting any one of these games. As the children notice that the activity has begun, they join in. After all the children are involved in the activity, we can move on to whatever we planned to do next.

Follow Me	Can You?
Arrows	Where Is...?
Clap Your Name	Bear or Lion Hunt
Old MacDonald Had a Body	Rhythmic Hand Patterns
Sounds to Move By	Wind, Rain, and Thunder

Calming-down activities

Is there a simple solution to an age-old problem? Wouldn't it be nice if we had some enjoyable activities that could bring children down from a hyperactive state without raising our voices or our blood pressure? Perhaps something that would refocus their attention and prepare them for what is going to happen next would be helpful.

Try some of the activities below. As the children become familiar with these activities, it may take no time at all for them to accept the challenge, join in, and recenter as a group—an "everybody wins" situation.

Follow Me (Have the final motions lead to a quiet position, such as
    sitting with hands folded.)
Can You? (Have the final challenge be one of quietness.)
I Am a Balloon (End with the balloon all collapsed and limp.)
Wind, Rain, and Thunder
Parts and Points
Bear or Lion Hunt
Jell-O Jiggle
Old MacDonald Had a Body
Rise and Shine
Letting Go

One key to using these as calming activities is how you bring the activity to an end.

Transition activities

After the following activities become familiar to the children, they can be done any time you have a few minutes.

Follow Me	Wind, Rain, and Thunder
Can You?	Arrows
Where Is...?	Busy Bee and Back to Back
Clap Your Name	Find It
Freeze	Memory Teaser
Mirroring	Parts and Points
Pop Up	Birds Fly
Sounds to Move By	Trying to Remember
Jell-O Jiggle	Old MacDonald Had a Body
Tiger, Tiger, Where's the Tiger?	Rise and Shine
Magic Jumping Beans	Body-Built Letters, Numbers, and
What Is Different?	Shapes

Small space activities and <u>really</u>* small space activities

Arrows*	Balloon Blow
Bear or Lion Hunt*	Birds Fly
What Is Different?*	Can You?*
Clap Your Name*	Follow Me*
Jell-O Jiggle	Magic Jumping Beans
Mirroring	Newspaper Delivery*
Parts and Points	Pop Up*
Sounds to Move By	Trying to Remember
Wind, Rain, and Thunder	Body-Built Letters, Numbers, and
	Shapes

Games that need enough space to form a circle

Balloon Keep Up	Birds Fly
Blanket Ball	Cross Over
Going on a Trip	Jell-O Jiggle
Meetball	Mirroring
Old MacDonald Had a Body	Pass the Shoe
Roll It	Rhythm Sticks
Sounds to Move By	Where Is...?
Where Is It?	The Winds Are Changing

Games that require space to spread out and move

Busy Bee and Back to Back	Body-Built Letters, Numbers,
Car and Driver	and Shapes
Carpet Activities	Cows and Ducks
Find It	Freeze
Help!	Islands
Rise and Shine	Robot
Squirrels in the Trees	Streamers
Tiger, Tiger, Where's the Tiger?	Weather Walks

A name game

Do you need to learn the names of your children? Do your children know each other's names? Do you need to help a new child enter the group? See "Meetball" and modifications.

Games for rainy or bad-weather days

When bad weather conditions prohibit outside play, try to find a large space if possible. The following games are listed in an order that we feel will help maintain some control while allowing the children needed physical activity.

Cross Over	The Winds Are Changing
Freeze	Busy Bee and Back To Back
Carpet Activities*	Islands
Squirrels in the Trees	Robot
Car and Driver	Rise and Shine
Streamers	Farmer-Farmer

*Carpet skates may make it possible to play actively in small spaces or reduce (see page 74) the injuries caused by children in larger spaces bumping into each other. It is helpful if the children have learned to use carpet skates prior to playing in a larger space. Hallways can be used for practice, or children may use carpet skates as they pass through the hall on their way to some specific destination.

It would also be nice if carpet skates could be made and placed in a box that is accessible to those using the large space.

If you choose to introduce a game that the children are not already familiar with, we would encourage you to initiate it in a limited area of the large space. You may want to use traffic cones or empty liter soda bottles to mark off this area.

In many situations we do not have the luxury of a large space. Consider playing the above games in the space available. When weather is bad and you have no large space to help children get rid of excess energy, you may need to play more games. Be careful that you don't attempt to counteract the children's need to move by making them sit too long and keep too quiet.

Starting new games

The games in this book were not developed to be played outside. Because there are so many wonderful distractions outside and because it can be hard to make yourself heard in such an open space, we would encourage you to initiate a new game inside. When it is well known and requires few words, you may want to consider using it to give structure to an outside play period that seems to be going nowhere or draw a play time to a conclusion to return to the inside. Children may choose to initiate a game or activity they have learned. This may be an indication that they wish to make this particular play period a social rather than a more exploratory play period (which can still be very social).

One should never forget that free play is a very important opportunity for the growing child. A playground or inside free play space should be equipped with possibilities that will help a child to initiate individual play. It is also a wonderful time for careful observation of children. Children send us many messages during their play time. The value of this time should never be underestimated.

Special needs children and children at risk

The philosophical difference between our progressive challenges and a stair-stepping, traditional progression may be a major key to being able to meet the needs of *all* children as they positively interact as a unified group. The inclusion factors of expansion, equalization and interactive challenge (page 3) also help.

Because children's special needs are as varied as the children themselves, we must make every effort to enable each child to participate at a personal level of social, emotional, cognitive, and physical growth.

26

The games in this book make this possible through the following characteristics:

- Each game is selected to help each participant gain a positive view of self and others.
- A broad range of differences can be accommodated.
- Continuous efforts have been made to reduce potential for emotional and social, as well as physical injury.
- The success or failure of an activity does not fall on the shoulders of any single individual or group.
- Errors are expected, can be self-evaluated, self-corrected, and are not externally judged.
- There is usually an almost instant opportunity to try again (to adjust, to repeat, to recover).
- Perseverance and coping with temporary frustration is encouraged by the format of the game.
- Self-control frequently contributes to achieving success.
- All of the components of the game tend to enhance the possibility of positive social interaction.
- No player is eliminated either blatantly or subtly.
- Joy, celebration, and fun are available to every participant.

The following games especially illustrate the characteristics listed above:

Islands
Bear or Lion Hunt
Old MacDonald Had a Body
Rise and Shine
Wind, Rain, and Thunder
Carpet Activities

Carpet skates may be used to increase the challenge and slow down speedsters participating in the following games:

Cross Over   Busy Bee and Back to Back
Car and Driver   Cows and Ducks
Help!   Find It
Robot   Squirrels in the Trees
The Winds Are Changing

Games have been continuously re-evaluated in relation to our philosophical approach to child development and to the characteristics of well-selected games, as stated above, making true mainstreaming increasingly possible.

Recommendations for Simplifications and Challenges are offered for many of the games. We encourage you to overcome the tendency to feel you must or ought to present a game as written. Since these games are tools (means), not ends in themselves, they can and should be changed to meet the players' needs. Use your experience and any professional assistance available to change the games in order to better serve the participants.

Perceptual motor abilities

What are perceptual motor abilities? Actually they are the end results of a very important process. Perceptual abilities are the means by which children perceive or take in their world, which includes themselves and all that is around them. Children perceive through their senses of sight, hearing, body sensations, timing, touch, and other senses. This sensory input—receiving the information—is the first step in children's learning.

There is also a very important second step. After information is taken in it must be interpreted. The process of making information meaningful occurs in the brain. The brain also stores information. It sorts out ideas and relates them to each other, making sense of perceptions. This is a relatively slow process. It takes many repetitions before our perceptions begin to make sense. It is important to appreciate that this is a slow and difficult process. We cannot assume that some children are being stubborn or lazy because they haven't gotten the idea yet.

These first two steps in the perceptual motor process require lots of input and repetition. This slow, repetitive process can bring energizing joy to the child or it can be agonizing, creating the need to withdraw or act out in disruptive ways. Our job is to bring joy and celebration to each child and to make positive self-esteem possible.

The *motor* part of perceptual motor abilities, or the third step, is the child's response (action taken or self-expression) in relation to what has been perceived and interpreted. This response gives us some indication of whether the first two steps have been effective. If there is an inappropriate response then we must decide what do to further support the first two steps.

Observe the child. There may be limitations or distractions that do not allow the child to take the first step. This could be anything from a limitation of one or more of the senses to an emotional fragmentation caused by frustration or external turmoil. Another possible difficulty could be in the processing system of step two. We are becoming increasingly aware that children can have learning disabilities that impede interpretation.

Some children may successfully complete the first two steps and still have difficulty in the third step. Children with cerebral palsy are an obvious example. Other children may have difficulties that are less obvious. Many times it is difficult to determine within which stage the processing has broken down, but we can help the child even though we cannot always pinpoint the origin of the difficulty. We have found that repetition of carefully selected experiences, continuously available progressive challenges, and a comfortable and empowering learning environment can support positive development in all three perceptual

Perceptual motor skills

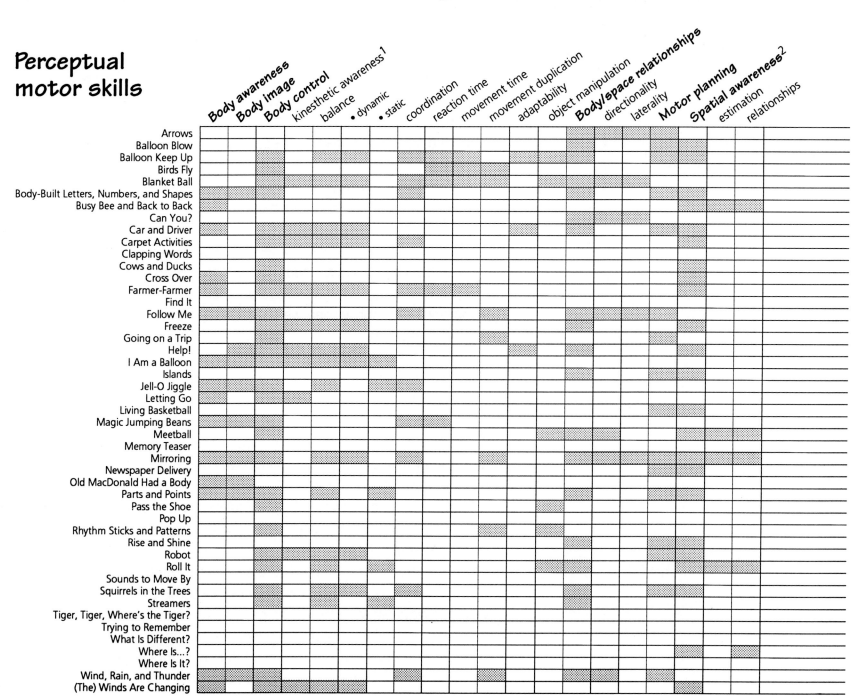

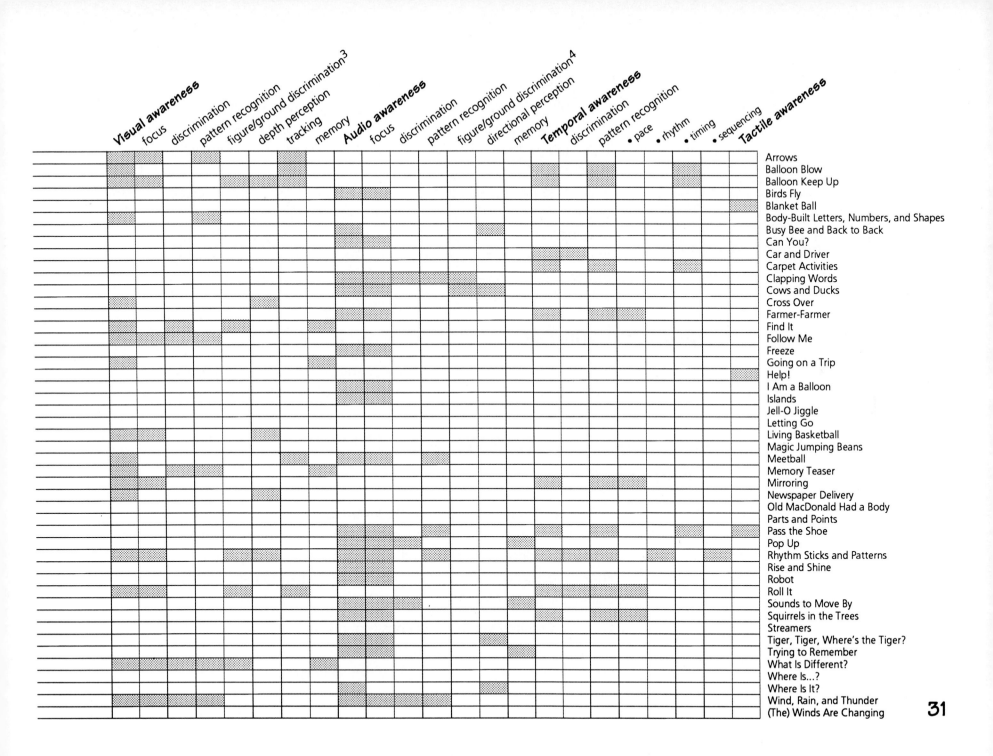

[1]Kinesthetic awareness is the ability to perceive your body positions from sensory messages received from end organs located in the muscles, tendons, and joints.

[2]Spatial awareness is an awareness of space, relative distance, and relationships within space.

[3]Visual figure/ground discrimination is the ability to separate and select a given relevant visual stimulus from competing irrelevant background.

[4]Auditory figure/ground discrimination is the ability to separate and select a given relevant auditory stimulus from competing irrelevant background sounds.

motor steps, increasing a child's ability to take in, interpret, and successfully respond. This is the process from which we learn.

Developing the abilities that will lead to lifetime success in this process is our job. Is it easy? No. But it is worth our effort, and can make a positive difference.

Because perceptual abilities are vital to daily functioning, you are encouraged to continue learning more about perceptual motor development and to relate this knowledge to activity selection. To help you select games, the chart on pages 30-31 tells you which perceptual motor skills are developed or reinforced in each game.

Hospitalized children

Note the list of games on page 47. Suggested games for hospitalized children are marked with an H to the right of the game name.

Children for whom English is their second language (ESL)

Play has always been considered a valuable tool in the development of expressive language. The simple group activities found within this book will allow children to interact initially without the need for an extensive English vocabulary. At the same time, many of the games can assist children in increasing their language base. Suggested games:

Arrows. Children say the directions (up, down, right, and left), allowing for lots of auditory input, practice in verbalizing the terms, and the development of an understanding of the concepts.

Bear or Lion Hunt. Children are given the opportunity to verbalize a growing number of familiar words as the action story is repeated over and over.

Birds Fly. Children match animal names with the concept of flying.

Body-Built Letters, Numbers, and Shapes. Children are given the opportunity to conceptualize and deal concretely with letters, numbers, and shapes.

Busy Bee and Back to Back. Children match body parts following verbal commands from leader.

Car and Driver. Children use terms such as *stop, go, slow, red light, green light, yellow light,* and perhaps even *caution.* Conceptualization of numbers as in *2 miles per hour, 5 miles per hour,* and so on, can be introduced.

Clapping Words. Children begin to hear words separated into syllables for auditory awareness, acuity, discrimination, pattern recognition, and auditory memory.

Cows and Ducks. Children practice auditory figure and ground discrimination.

Find It. Children recognize words related to colors, numbers, objects, animals, words, or other teacher-selected items.

Freeze. Children conceptualize a single word *(freeze)* that may increase safety.

Going on a Trip. Children participate in multiple verbal repetitions related to specific common objects as well as classmates' names while receiving both visual and auditory support from other members of the group.

Help! The words *thank you* and *you are welcome* could be incorporated into this game for extra language practice.

Jell-O Jiggle. Children identify body parts.

Meetball. Children learn other children's names and participate in a group shout.

Memory Teaser. Children are motivated to express themselves in giving physical responses to spoken challenges.

Old MacDonald Had a Body. Children practice verbalization while learning body parts.

Parts and Points. Children learn specific body part names.

Rhythmic Hand Patterns. Verbalization of numbers and letters could be included in this game.

What Is Different? Children are motivated to express themselves in giving answers.

Where Is...? Children relate specific words and objects.

getting families involved in play

Family members need quality time together. Reality sometimes works against this, and parents often realize too late that the years have robbed them of this very special opportunity. Perhaps you can help by providing opportunities for parents or guardians to share special times (even brief ones) with their children. Making a piece of junk equipment together, with which the child can then continue to play, extends the hours of connectedness between adult and child. The piece of junk equipment also acts as a reminder of the experience each time the child plays with it. In the back of this book, in the section entitled, "Making Equipment At Little Or No Cost," there are ideas that can be copied and sent home to families.

You might also send a note home encouraging parents or guardians to ask children to show them how to play a particular game. Or hold a family night at which the adults join the children in playing games. A workshop to explain, experience, and better understand the value of these games may encourage parents to become more supportive and actively involved with their child's play. This might give additional clout to your program and at the same time give parents a better idea of what their children are gaining. Suggested letters are provided below.

Letter to parents or primary care provider

Dear _____ ,

Games and homemade equipment can be fun as well as enriching. Addison-Wesley Publishing Company has given us permission to copy and send the enclosed games and low-cost equipment ideas home to you. They are from Follow Me Too: A Handbook of Movement Activities for Three- to Five-Year-Olds. *We hope you have as much fun playing them with your child as we do.*

Sincerely,

A pre-holiday letter

Dear _____ ,

During the holiday your children may have some extra time to play. There may be gatherings of relatives or friends where groups of children will be together. Addison-Wesley Publishing Company has given us permission to copy and send the enclosed games and low-cost equipment ideas home to you. They are from Follow Me Too: A Handbook of Movement Activities for Three- to Five-Year-Olds. *We hope you will find them to be fun, entertaining, and enriching.*

Sincerely,

Letter to a hospitalized or recovering child's family

Dear _____ ,

We have missed _____. We are looking forward to (her/his) return. We are enclosing a few games and ideas for homemade equipment that might be fun.

   Please give _____ a hug from all of us.

Sincerely,

You may even want to consider having a "Pre-Holiday Family Get-Together Workshop" to play and make some low cost equipment.

For each of the three letters select some junk equipment items from "Making Equipment at Little or No Cost" that the adults could make with the child, some games from the list below, or some hospital games (marked with an H). Duplicate the entire game, including "Life Skills," to allow parents to become aware of the value of the activities you do with their child.

The following activities are favorites of the authors and might serve as a guide in selecting games for parents to begin with.

Follow Me (H)	Can You? (H)
Balloon Blow (H)	Carpet Activities
Arrows (H)	Where Is...? (H)
Clapping Words (H)	Memory Teaser (H)
Mirroring (H)	Sounds to Move By (H)
Trying to Remember (H)	Jell-O Jiggle (H)
Old MacDonald Had a Body (H)	Washing Machine
Body-Built Letters, Numbers, and Shapes	What Is Different? (H)
Newspaper Delivery	Find It

building self-esteem

In the authors' experience, building an environment that facilitates the development of self-esteem is probably the single most powerful and energizing gift you can give to the young child.

In a pilot study completed by Lynne B. Schneider in 1989, it was found that for kindergartners who learned and played games from *Follow Me: A Handbook of Movement Activities for Children* (elementary school version of *Follow Me Too*), improvement of self-esteem was statistically significant; a control group that participated only in the regular free play period did not show this improvement.

This study does not negate free play from which children gain valuable benefits other than measurable self-esteem. But it does demonstrate that carefully selected games and activities may have a positive effect on a child's self-regard. This would seem reasonable, since the games in *Follow Me* that are developed by the Leonard Gordon Institute for Human Development Through Play of Temple University are predicated on factors meant to contribute to this end result.

facilitating growth

Every effort has been made to see that that the games and activities found in this book are developmentally appropriate for 3- to 5-year-olds.

The selection, modification, and development of the games and activities presented in this book are based upon two evaluation processes. A game is considered for inclusion only if it passes both of these evaluative processes. The first evaluation process analyzes the life skills being practiced within a game. To be an acceptable game, it has to facilitate the development of one or more important life skills. The second evaluation process determines whether the structure of the game allows each participant choices to enter at a personal level of social, emotional, cognitive, and physical growth. This approach is based on the work of Robert W. White of Harvard. It proposes that human beings have an innate drive toward efficacy, competency, mastery and growth; thus a child will reach for growth whenever it is available. Our task is to offer games and activities that support and facilitate that availability.

using volunteers to help in your games program

Volunteers can be most helpful in implementing your games program. Because the games are straightforward, volunteers can read about them and help children play them or simply direct and supervise if the children already know the games. By having them read the "Life Skills" and "Comments and Suggestions" sections, you are also educating volunteers to a deeper understanding of what you are all about. Volunteers may want to go back and examine "Simplifications and Challenges" for additional ideas.

It is also extremely helpful to have volunteers make, repair, or replace the equipment described in "Making Equipment at Little or No Cost" starting on page 154. Volunteers can also make extras to be sent home with children for home play. Remember, whatever life skills are being practiced while playing each game and using each piece of equipment contribute to the child's growth because of your program and its extended seed-planting effort.

intergenerational play

As we are well aware, senior citizens and young children can establish special relationships. Seek out the older volunteer and use the simple games and activities to facilitate intergenerational interactions. Consider the following:

"Making Equipment at Little or No Cost"

yarn balls	trash balls
racket and balloon	milk jug scoops

Mirroring
Balloon Keep Up (One-on-One)
What Is Different?
Where Is...?
Wind, Rain, and Thunder

how to avoid out-of-control play

If control is a problem for any member of your staff some of the following suggestions might help:

- Read "Some Thoughts About Preschoolers," especially 2 and 3 on pages 10–12.
- Teach children games that allow them to learn and practice self-control.
- Have adults model aspects of the game and then have only a few children at a time try it while the rest watch; continue to increase the number of children active at one time, until all children are participating.
- Evaluate whether the children are bored or not understanding what they are to do.
- Consider whether the children are being asked to sit too long when they are not actively involved.
- Work with a smaller group before teaching the activity to the entire group.

what to look for
in a game

Inclusion

Does the game include everyone? Eliminate elimination rather than players. Being included in a game helps a player develop a sense of belonging and importance.

The focus is off failure

Does the game encourage the players to try (maybe even risk) again and again without feeling as though they have failed? No one likes to fail, especially if the opportunity to try again is not made available. Games that encourage players to try either again or in different ways in a safe environment help players develop a sense of confidence and perseverance and a willingness to try or to take risks.

Each player is allowed to enter in at her or his own level

Does the game offer both the unskilled and the skilled player an opportunity to be an integral, contributing member? Does the game allow both the unskilled and skilled player an opportunity to learn from each other and contribute to one another's growth? Being able to learn from one another and also to contribute to one another's growth help develop confidence as well as team building and group bonding. At the same time, autonomy is fostered.

All players are sharing in a challenging experience

Does the game enable each player to make a contribution to the challenge of the game? (The above-mentioned factors help to create this setting.) When all players are working together toward the challenge of the game, a sense of togetherness and bonding will be created.

The environment is safe socially, emotionally, and physically

Is the game threatening socially, emotionally, or physically? Is there the potential for someone to get hurt socially, emotionally, or physically? Could any of these injuries happen subtly rather than overtly? The person who is selecting and leading a game must look out for these injuries in an effort to prevent, minimize, or defuse them.

Adapting games to fit children's needs

A "Comments and Suggestions" section has been included with each game to help you expand the use of the game and adapt it to the needs of your group.

Most programs list games by ages. This book deliberately avoids this practice. Two factors determine the age appropriateness of an activity: the leader's approach to the activity and the progressive challenges available within each activity.

Both of these can effectively be applied by the leader, who can select and modify games according to the group. The Simplifications and Challenges section may assist in this process and help in creating new versions of the basic games.

Because it is important to be aware of the needs met by games, Life Skills are listed at the beginning of each game.

Be aware that all games can be adjusted to your group by increasing or decreasing the challenge level. Asking your group if they believe they are ready to handle a more difficult challenge motivates them to increase their focus, which leads to greater self-control. As your group becomes accustomed to being asked if they are ready to accept a new challenge, you may focus them further by asking, "Are you sure?"

games

Games are listed alphabetically.

An (H) beside the name of the game indicates that this game could be used in a hospital setting.

Arrows (H)

Balloon Blow (H)

Balloon Keep Up (H)

Bear or Lion Hunt (H)

Birds Fly (H)

Blanket Ball

Body-Built Letters, Numbers, and
    Shapes

Busy Bee and Back to Back

Can You? (H)

Car and Driver

Carpet Activities

Clapping Words (H)

Cows and Ducks

Cross Over

Farmer-Farmer

Find It

Follow Me (H)

Freeze (H)

Going on a Trip (H)

Help!

I am a Balloon (H)

Islands

Jell-O Jiggle (H)

Letting Go (H)

Lion or Bear Hunt (H)

Living Basketball (H)

Magic Jumping Beans (H)

Meetball (H)

Memory Teaser (H)

Mirroring (H)

Newspaper Delivery

Old MacDonald Had a Body (H)

Parts and Points (H)

Pass the Shoe

Pop Up

Rhythm Sticks and Rhythmic
    Hand Patterns

Rise and Shine (H)

Robot

Roll It

Silly Name Game (in Meetball)

Simon Says (in Birds Fly)

Sounds to Move By (H)

Squirrels in the Trees

Streamers (H)

Tiger, Tiger, Where's the Tiger? (H)

Trying to Remember

Weather Walks (H)

What Is Different? (H)

Where Is. . .? (H)

Where Is It? (H)

Wind, Rain, and Thunder (H)

The Winds are Changing (H)

arrows (H)

Life Skills
- Focusing attention, concentrating, increasing attention span
- Recognizing patterns
- Decoding and translating information from symbols
- Reinforcing *up, down, left, right*
- Duplicating visual patterns
- Following auditory instructions (Simplifications and Challenges)
- Making decisions
- Developing mental flexibility and adaptability
- Practicing self-evaluation
- Functioning under stress
- Having fun
- Getting the idea; putting factors together (discovery) without adult evaluative intervention

Materials
- A large chart or chalkboard showing four arrows:

  up ↑   down ↓   left ←   right →

Directions
Display the four directional arrows so that all players can clearly see them. As you point to an arrow, all are to move both their arms in that direction. You may want to start slowly in sequence, but then gradually increase the challenge level by pointing a little faster. After each move to a new arrow, pause to give everyone a chance to participate. This pause allows all the players to process information at their own pace or level and feel successful. Rushing to the next arrow increases excitement, but rushing on too soon can leave some children frustrated and with a sense

of failure. Pausing is a very important technique. Later you may choose to point to the arrows out of sequence. Your pace and challenge level is best determined by the responses from your group. Errors will occur. It is important that the players realize that it is fun to try; make them comfortable with the idea that this is a game and that mistakes are OK and expected. This climate comes about more from your attitude (which is felt by the children) than from any spoken words.

Comments and Suggestions

- Players can sit or stand. Standing gives them more freedom of movement but may make it harder to see the arrows.
- Have all players move into a position where they can see the arrows and will be able to reach out without bumping one another.
- If possible allow children to choose where they want to stand, allowing them to process information more effectively.
- Your enjoyment in leading this activity can add to the fun of it.
- Some activities allow children to put factors within their experience together over time in a *discovery* manner. This is empowering to a child, building autonomy (self-determination, self-governance, self-evaluation). Because it may involve a period of fumbling (discovering), adults can be too empathetic and want to direct the children to the answer(s), thus reducing this opportunity to experience the ability to overcome a difficult challenge. Our task is to engineer the environment so that the child can experience this discovery process.
- A smile from you when children are making an effort can mean a lot to them.
- Very young participants simply enjoy trying to meet the challenge and may need more time. Move slowly and be sure that there is enough time for all to try. Don't correct errors. Give children plenty of turns and they'll begin to catch on. Remember, their experience may be limited. For some players the first simple version is all they need.

- This game may later help children recognize the difference between *b, d, g, p,* and *q* more easily.
- As participants become more familiar with the activity, they may need to feel more challenged. But they still need time to process information and succeed. Don't overlook the importance of the pause, and remember that success is fun. A game is meant to be fun, so try to allow as many as possible to feel like winners.

Simplifications and Challenges

- As a lead in, ask children, "Can you reach up, down, to this side, to this other side?" as you model each position.
- Rather than using the arrows, move your arms in the four directions and have players try to move their arms accordingly. Later you might have the children attempt to say the direction as they move to each new position. If some have problems with *left* and *right,* you may first want to use *side.* Remember that when you are facing the group you will have to say "right" when you are actually moving left to make it correct.
- Have the group say the direction *(up, down, left, right)* when they move their arms. This is more difficult than just moving.
- In each of these versions you may eventually want to consider having the children identify and say the directions by themselves. You simply do the motion while the players do the motion and say the direction.
- You simply say the direction and the children attempt to move accordingly, thus changing this from an activity of visual focus and concentration to an auditory one.

Thanks to Tom Cleland and his understanding of learning disabilities in trying to help us build a better set of challenges for this activity.

balloon blow[H]

Life Skills
- Developing the concept of air movement and its effects
- Recognizing that one can have an effect on the environment (this is subtle but very important)
- Beginning to interact with cause-and-effect thinking
- Planning in relation to cause and effect
- Developing a sense of timing in relation to a changing external environment
- Learning to adapt one's plan as the environment changes
- Practicing concentration, attention, perseverance, visual focus, visual tracking skills
- Practicing respiratory control and development
- Developing spatial awareness (an awareness of space, relative distance, and relationships within space)
- Practicing self-control
- Working with others

Materials
- Cotton balls, balloons, or large, lightweight objects that can be blown around
- A straw for each player (you may be able to cut each straw in half or roll paper to form a straw)

Directions
Players sit around a table. A cotton ball, balloon, or a large, lightweight object is placed in the center of the table. The whole group is asked to attempt to blow this object around the table. After accomplishing this challenge they try blowing the object to every player at the table.

- Keep an eye open for signs of hyperventilation as children get really involved.
- A balloon slows the pace of the activity, but does not usually seem to reduce the challenge for the players.
- Think about whether the children will be able to enjoy their ability to control whatever object(s) you have selected.
- Be observant. If some children do not get the balloon very often, a challenge might be, "Can we get it down to this end of the table?"
- Occasionally an assertive child will unconsciously reach out to prevent nearby players from blowing. If this occurs or if you feel it might occur, simply have all children hold their straws with both hands.
- Some play this activity after lunch when straws may be available. It can involve those children who are finished with their lunches and encourage the rest of the children to finish their lunches in order to play.
- Remember that balloons and balloon fragments can be hazardous.

Simplifications and Challenges

- For an individual child you may want to set up a target, such as an empty plastic soda bottle. Tie a balloon so that it hangs down and could touch or perhaps even knock the bottle over when blown. The degree of challenge can be changed by changing the position of the bottle in relation to the hanging balloon and the path it can take, changing the weight and number of the objects to be hit, or putting a little water in the balloon. With two children, one could be the guard and attempt to prevent (by blowing) the balloon from hitting the bottle (or knocking it over), while the other player attempts to make a point by hitting it or perhaps two points by knocking it over.
- You could establish an obstacle course or zig-zag path on a table or tray and have children blow a cotton ball through the obstacle course. You might include paths, bridges, tunnels, and so on.
- The players could attempt to blow the object the full length of the table and into a wastepaper basket or large box on the floor at the end.

balloon keep up[H]

Life Skills
- Practicing self-control
- Handling stress
- Concentrating and focusing on purpose
- Persevering
- Monitoring the changing environment
- Practicing visual tracking (following an object as it travels through space)
- Practicing visual figure and ground discrimination (the ability to separate the relevant from the irrelevant in the visual field in order to focus on the relevant)
- Sensing one's ability to have an effect on one's environment
- Sharing and helping
- Making multiple rapid, minor decisions
- Learning (intuiting) the effects of various contact points on an object

Materials
- Lots of colorful balloons at least 7–8 inches in diameter

Directions

Children keep balloons from touching the floor. Young children find that simply keeping the balloon in the air is fun. You may want to have them sit on the floor, since they do not have the body and space awareness to move around the area without bumping into each other.

Comments and Suggestions
- Over-inflated balloons are apt to break more easily, which can frighten a very young player.
- The number of balloons used changes the stress level, the number of turns available, and the degree of self-control needed. You will need to evaluate and re-evaluate this as you play this game with your children.

- Remember that balloons and balloon fragments can be hazardous.
- Two players, such as a senior citizen and a child, can play together. This is called "One-on-One."

Simplifications and Challenges

- Play "Poke Ball" by marking a face on a large, light-colored trash bag. Blow up the bag and tie it off so that the air cannot escape. The objective is to keep the bag in the air. You may have to help the children realize that they must be gentle, poking rather than hitting this homemade balloon.
- You might try using the nylon stocking and wire coathanger racket with a balloon attached. Directions for making the racket can be found in the equipment section.
- Divide the class into two groups. One group (perhaps the younger or more inexperienced children if your group varies in age or abilities) sits on the floor cross-legged or in any position that will keep them sitting. The other group (your helpers) stands in a circle around them. If adults or older children are playing, it might be helpful to ask them to be in this outer circle. This group should be one giant step back from the first group to prevent them from hitting balloons that are still within the first group's reach. If you feel that your outer circle cannot hold this position you may want to have them sit in chairs. Those sitting inside the circle will attempt to keep all the balloons as high in the air as possible. Those in the outer circle hit the balloons back into the center of the circle when they escape. Later you may want to change the two groups.

Thanks to Michael Schneider for the "Poke Ball" variation.
Thanks to Dr. Ira Shapiro of Temple University's Recreation and Leisure Department for putting this combination together for inventing the inner and outer circles variation.

bear or lion hunt^(H)

Life Skills
- Developing memory skills
- Focusing attention and concentration
- Being part of a group, having fun with others
- Making decisions
- Making a contribution
- Dealing with suspense and excitement; self-control
- Handling stress

Materials   No special materials are needed.

Directions   The leader tells an action story in which everything said by the story teller is repeated by the players. For example:

> *Let's go on a lion hunt!* (players repeat)
> *Ready? Let's go!* (players repeat)

Add details and obstacles as you go (bridge, tall grass, river, swamp and so on):

> *I see a bridge.* (players repeat)
> *Can't go around it.* (players repeat)
> *Can't go under it.* (players repeat)
> *Might as well go over it.* (players repeat)

Children slap alternate thighs with hands to represent walking.
This action continues throughout the entire story except when other movements are used or when the story does not involve walking.

All kinds of events can be used to create your own story. The following are just samples.

- going out of a gate (swing it shut after you)
- going over a bridge (sound can be made by gently thumping one's chest)
- going through tall grass (making the motion of parting the grass)
- swimming across a river
- sloshing through a swamp
- sneaking quietly past a sleeping animal
- climbing up a tree
- looking through field glasses
- seeing a faraway cave in the side of a mountain
- climbing down the tree
- traveling to a mountain
- climbing the mountain
- discovering that the cave is dark
- feeling along the damp wall of the cave
- finding something very sharp
- realizing that the very sharp thing is a tooth
- being chased (reverse all previous actions)
- wiping one's forehead
- arriving home, jumping over the gate, slamming the door, giving a big sigh of relief

Give each new part of the story an appropriate action and sound effect.

Comments and Suggestions

- This activity can be done sitting or standing.
- This can be used as a transition activity.
- Begin with a short story. Increase the length and complexity of actions as players become proficient at the game.
- Don't expect the trip to be perfect; players will enjoy the game even if mistakes are made.

- When players learn the basic format they can add new stories and action ideas.
- Reversing the order of events may be too difficult for preschoolers. Simply have the children follow along with you. It may also be difficult for you, but having a list posted where you can see it may help.
- Players with limited movement can also participate in this activity.
- A sense of group unity is developed in this activity; everyone in the group participates together.

Simplifications and Challenges

- If the players have visited a zoo, amusement park, or museum, an action story might be a good way to review what they have seen.
- Calm down the excitement level by ending the activity on a quiet note:

  Close the door.
  Close your eyes.
  Think about the animal that was chasing you. Where has it gone? What is it doing?

- Use different animals and settings to create stories and actions.

Thanks to Sheila Kaufman for the calming suggestions to end the activity.

birds fly (H)

Life Skills
- Making decisions (the development of the ability to make major life decisions can be initiated at a very young age; by encouraging myriad opportunities to make minor decisions that are of a less serious nature an individual can begin to learn about the process)
- Practicing self-evaluation
- Classifying/categorizing

Materials

No special materials are needed.

Directions

Ask the children if they can name some things that fly. Then have everyone stand. Name a series of objects and animals, including things that fly. Each time you name anything that flies, the players flap their arms vigorously (for instance, "ducks fly" and "mosquitoes fly"). If you name something that does not fly, all the players should cross their arms across their chests.

Comments and Suggestions
- As the children become familiar with the game and with what flies and what doesn't, players might become leaders; a player who seems to understand the concept of the activity probably could be the first leader.
- You will find some discrepancy in players' responses; Dumbo the elephant can fly, as can other storybook characters.
- This good quick activity can be used almost anywhere, giving restless children a chance to move. Parents might appreciate this as a suggestion for getting rid of the fidgets on long car trips.

- Those who have difficulty will probably begin by taking the late but more obvious visual input from other players, but as the activity progresses, most players will be challenged by the independence allowed by the verbal input.
- In a limited space players can bend their arms, put their fingers under their armpits and flap their wings.
- Notice that those who fail are not eliminated.
- This might be a good preliminary activity to "Simon Says" (see below).
- If you wish to encourage players to attend to auditory input, challenge them to try to play with their eyes closed.

Simplifications and Challenges

- "Simon Says" is similar to "Birds Fly." The leader says, "Simon says" followed by an action—"stand up"; "reach high"; "clap hands." The participants do everything that Simon says, but if an action direction is not preceded by "Simon says," players do not follow the direction. To allow the children to process their decisions, go slowly. Do not eliminate players; every player needs the growth and development experiences available in participation. Let children self-evaluate, self-correct, and go on. If they do not self-evaluate and self-correct, they simply may not be ready to do so. Let them play and observe over time. Our experience has been that repeated experiences do not spoil the excitement of the game. Trying to figure it out is fun in and of itself and leads to growth and further willingness to risk.

Thanks to Pam Scott for the "flying in a limited space" variation of "Birds Fly."

blanket ball

Life Skills
- Interacting cooperatively with others to accomplish a common goal or challenge
- Practicing self-control
- Solving problems
- Developing spatial awareness (an awareness of space, relative distance, and relationships within space)
- Learning to anticipate and predict
- Practicing cognitive skills

Materials
- A plain bedsheet without designs, or some other light material that is large enough for the whole group to participate
- Objects such as cardboard cutouts, old socks, balloons, yarn balls

Directions

The group arranges itself around the sheet and sits down. Begin with a sock so that children can get the idea of the game; have them practice lifting the sock on the sheet on the count of three. Then move to a cardboard disk that is about 6 inches in diameter and has a different color on each side. Place this disk in the center of the sheet. Please note "Comments and Suggestions" below.

The following steps can be presented one at a time. When you feel that one has been successfully conquered, move on to the next.

- Have children work together and try to lift the sheet all at the same time on the count of three and then gently lower it. Have them take hold of the sheet. Make sure everyone is ready. Slowly count to three. (A secret: announce the final three very calmly and softly or the children may become over-stimulated.) You may want the group to count with you. Practice several times just lifting the sheet and bringing it gently back down, until the group has conquered this challenge. Then decide whether your group is ready to go on.

- Place a two-sided disk with a different color on each side on the sheet. Have children very gently lift the disk from the sheet and then gently catch it and stop it. On the count of three, they gently lift together.

  1. Have children predict which side of the colored disk will come up.
  2. Lift and stop the sheet again and see which side comes down.
  3. Repeat the steps.

If children have exhibited self-control through this series, you might choose to move on. If control has been difficult or impossible for them to maintain, it may be best to put the activity away for now. If children ask for it later, remind them how difficult it is before they try again.

A flat sock will not go too high, damage anything, or hurt anyone, allowing the children to see how high they can lift the sock and still catch it when it comes down. For now, start by asking the children if they can work together, lift the sock up off the sheet, and catch it as it comes down. If they handle this well or they find themselves frustrated because they want the sock to go higher, you might choose to tie one loose knot in the middle of the sock. This concentrates the weight and makes it possible to lift the sock higher with the same amount of force.

For some groups a balloon is just too exciting or difficult to keep on the sheet. You may want to offer this as a very difficult challenge, but be ready to prevent the situation from escalating toward chaos by returning to the sock or ending the activity before it gets out of hand.

Comments and Suggestions

- You may want to have the group set the sheet neatly on the floor and then sit down around it. Since this can be a very exciting activity and can get out of control if each step isn't carefully controlled, each time

61

you wish to talk to the children you might have them place the sheet carefully on the floor. If the children are getting too excited, you may want to play "Follow Me" or "Can You?" for a few rounds to calm them down before returning to "Blanket Ball."

- You may want to divide the class into smaller groups. Choose appropriate objects for each group.
- Having children grip the sheet with their thumbs above and their fingers underneath makes them less apt to grab at whatever is on the sheet. This may very subtly add to impulse control.
- You may need to go about this activity slowly and calmly. It might help to begin with a statement such as, "This is a difficult activity and we may not be able to do it, but I'd like to try. If it is too hard we'll put it away and try it again later in the year. Would you like to try it?" Some teachers have the children think of the sheet as a soft wind or the ocean or use a feather as the object to be lifted.
- The objects you use on the sheet could be labeled with alphabet letters, numbers, colors, and so on. A labeled prop in the shape of a fish can be used; the sheet is the water. The fish jumps up out of the water and may turn over when it comes down. The children can all call out the letter, number, or color when the fish lands in the water again.
- This activity seems to develop a sense of group unity and focus.
- Some have found that children who do not always participate in other games or don't understand how to play other games can enter in and be a part of this game. This is very special group dynamics.
- It is fun for children to say "hello" to each other as they raise the sheet.
- This is a good game for hot days; the moving material can fan the players.
- You may want gradually to add to the complexity of this activity over time.

62

- The time placement of this activity in the day's schedule could prove to be a very important factor. You may want to use a calm-down activity if your group is hyped at the end.
- Terry Orlick's *Cooperative Sports and Games* may be a book you'd like to take a look at.

Simplifications and Challenges

- Sitting on the floor seems to increase self-control. Sitting in chairs may increase self-control even further.
- Sitting in chairs also helps when you have children and adults participating.
- Have the children make the sound of a particular letter as it lands on the sheet.
- Two socks may be used, one that is knotted and the other flat. Have the children predict which will go higher.
- Add music.

Thanks to Mary Ellen Hence for the suggestion of having children grip the sheet with their thumbs above it and fingers below, and also having the children say "hello" as they raise the sheet.

It was Marilyn Khan's idea to use a prop in the shape of a fish and pretend that the sheet is the water.

The flat and knotted socks suggestion came from Geneva Szatny.

body-built letters, numbers, and shapes

Life Skills

- Seeking for and recognizing patterns—this allows a child to become more aware that lines and curves help form symbols and have meanings; interpretation of symbols is based on awareness of patterns and relationships

Materials

No special materials are needed.

Directions

Have the players try to form letters, numbers, or shapes with their own bodies or with a partner.

Comments and Suggestions

- Some children may wish to lie on the floor to form letters or numbers or shapes.
- Get children started by suggesting letters, numbers, or shapes for them to form. Good letters to start with are *I, T, Y,* and *C* (*C* usually has to be done on the floor).
- Personal meaning can be brought to this activity by having players attempt to do one of their initials.
- Remember that you may get many kinds of responses. Try to perceive how the child sees her or his answer as a particular letter or number. This may also give you some important clues as to specific difficulties.
- Sometimes a child who seems to be just watching is also learning.

64

© Addison-Wesley Publishing Company, Inc.

Simplifications and Challenges

- Display pictures of letters, numbers, or shapes.
- Have the children trace the form with a finger before attempting to make it with their bodies.
- A sand table may be helpful to practice making the various forms.
- Form a letter, number, or shape on the floor with string or rope. The children can then form it with their bodies.
- Have the children work in twos, threes, or fours; challenge them to include everyone.

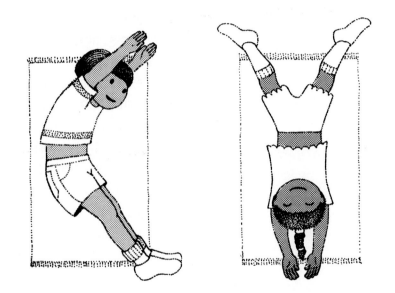

busy bee and back to back

Life Skills
- Listening carefully
- Remaining alert
- Making multiple, simple decisions; having to change one's mind quickly if an initial plan does not work
- Assuming responsibility for not bumping another
- Practicing body control and moving effectively when all are hurrying and scurrying about
- Remaining in emotional control while dealing with a high stimulation level, rapid changes, and active physical involvement
- Interacting comfortably with a great number of others (because of rapid changes of partners and the back-to-back position, players are less apt to seek out their friends; a shy or less popular participant is not as apt to be left out or chosen last)

Materials   No special materials are needed.

Directions   Each time the leader calls "Busy Bee," all players begin buzzing. A player stops buzzing when he or she finds another player and stands back to back. If an extra player cannot find a partner, you can stand back to back with this player. "Busy Bee" is called again, and buzzing players find new partners. You may want to challenge the players to find a different partner every time. (Be aware that in this version some players may eventually realize that they are with someone they have already had as a partner. When they announce this, you may have to ask the group if there is any way to help these players. At first this may be confusing, but it can support the concept of helping others.)

Comments and Suggestions

- Start with the children in a group, rather than having them choose partners before the game starts. Let the first call of "Busy Bee" begin the game.
- Sometimes three or four young children will all stand back to back together. This is fine unless you wish them to do otherwise.
- Changing partners frequently seems to help prevent children from choosing only certain other children.
- This activity reduces the chances of not being chosen. *Be sensitive to the effect that various aspects of games and activities can have on players and make selections and challenges accordingly.*
- Try not to emphasize who is last. Encourage children to help each other find a free bee. Continuing to try helps children learn to persevere.
- This is usually a good time to observe children. What is the social interaction of your group? Does any participant have difficulty with this activity? Why? Use the information to help you select other games that will help children grow.
- When the children are familiar with this game you may want to use a few "Busy Bee" calls to divide the group into partners for other games or group happenings. By using several calls of "Busy Bee" you mix the group better and reduce the possibility of a child being chosen last or being left out.

Simplifications and Challenges

- When the group is ready for a new challenge, you may choose to make calls such as "back to back," "knee to knee," "palms to palms," and so on. (Since passing head lice is a possibility, avoid calls such as "head to head.") Children may enjoy "Touch your fingers with your friend's fingers," and "Touch your friend's toes with your toes."

Vary the degree of simplicity or complexity in this activity according to your group. This can change over time.

Thanks to Jackie Hersh for suggesting "Touch your fingers with your friend's fingers," and so on.

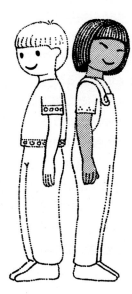

68

can you?(H)

Life Skills

- Auditory focusing, attending, and concentrating with distractions (personal movement involvement + the noise and movement of others)
- Careful listening, which leads to being able to accept a challenge
- Decoding the spoken word
- Learning to follow verbal instructions
- Accepting a challenge
- Problem solving
- Being able to know and manipulate one's body in order to function effectively in various situations
- Persevering

Materials

No special materials are needed.

Directions

Players respond to the "Can you?" challenge of the leader. Examples include reach high, stand up, sit down, turn around, hide, place your elbow higher than your ear. See also "Some Thoughts About Preschoolers," page 10.

Comments and Suggestions

- After each "Can You?" try to pause in order for everyone to participate. This pause allows children to process information at their own pace or level and feel successful. Rushing to the next challenge contributes to the excitement, but rushing on too soon can frustrate some children and leave them with a sense of failure. This is a very important technique.
- Consider not repeating a "Can you?" question. A child who has difficulty responding to the first auditory challenge may need to

become aware that unless you are auditorily alert you may miss something. This child can take visual clues from other children and then be auditorily ready for the next call.

- This activity can be used as quick challenges almost anywhere or any time or in any number to change the pace or meet other needs.
- The activity may be used to get the children's attention.
- If children are familiar with "Follow Me," begin by doing the movement you are asking of the children. Gradually reduce your participation, giving only verbal cues.
- "Can You?" can be a calming-down activity if you end with calming challenges: "Can you lie down?" and "Can you go to sleep?"

Simplifications and Challenges

- If you wish to encourage players to attend to auditory input you might challenge them to try to do this with their eyes closed.
- As a year-long challenge, have children repeat a sequence.
- Suggest challenges with partners: "Can you touch your fingers with your friend's fingers?" and "Can you touch your friend's toes with your toes?"
- Have children participate in a variation called Magic Circling—"Can you find a large red object and walk slowly around it?" "Can you find something we slide down and walk around it?"

"Can You?" allows a child to risk and accept a challenge. If unable to conquer the challenge immediately, the child can choose to try again, learning that effort can lead to improvement. A direct command ("Do this"), too frequently leaves the child with a feeling of success or failure and a self-evaluation of "I can—I am able" or "I can't—I am inadequate," rather than an attitude that trying and perseverance pay off.

Thanks to Jackie Hersh for the suggestion of telling children to "touch your fingers with your friend's fingers," and so on.

car and driver

Life Skills
- Maintaining attention and focus under distracting conditions
- Accepting responsibility for another
- Practicing self-control by not running your partner into someone else
- Developing spatial awareness (an awareness of space, relative distance, and relationships within space)
- Making decisions
- Being trustworthy
- Being sensitive to someone else's fear or hesitancy
- Building trust in others
- Learning to lead and follow
- Using one's imagination

Materials

No special materials are needed.

Directions

Players have partners. One (the driver) stands behind the other (the car). The cars may feel more comfortable if they are allowed to put their arms out in front of them (as safety bumpers). The drivers direct, stop, and start the cars using only their hands, which are placed upon their partners' shoulders or waist (car's choice). Players later change roles. Red light, green light, and speed limits can be introduced.

Comments and Suggestions

- "Cross Over" and "Freeze" may be good preliminary activities to introduce before this one.

Simplifications and Challenges

- Have preschoolers play "Horse and Buggy." Players don't hold on to each other. They pretend to hold the reins and follow one another.
- Suggest scenarios to control the action, such as cars stuck in traffic, cars on a bumpy road, and so on.
- Play "Cross Over." Do the activity in slow motion (5 MPH) or on carpet skates, or cardboard pieces. Use "Carpet Activities," page 77.
- Specify that if two cars touch, an accident has occurred and they cannot move from the scene, creating an obstacle for other drivers to go around. A person (you or another child must touch the car—report and repair) before it is to move again.

> Sharon Harrison wanted her players to go slowly and with self-control, so she made up a story about them being expensive antique cars in a show.
> Thanks to Sherry McBride for the "Horse and Buggy" suggestion.

carpet activities

Life Skills
- Practicing balance and total body coordination
- Developing kinesthetic awareness (ability to perceive one's body positions from sensory messages received from end organs located in the muscles, tendons, and joints)
- Developing an active life style
- Learning to enjoy a vigorous workout
- Improving cardiovascular development
- Improving abdominal development
- Learning to respect differences and discovering that one can enjoy others who are different
- Developing spatial awareness (an awareness of space, relative distance, and relationships within space)
- Persevering
- Practicing self-evaluation
- Getting the idea, putting factors together (discovery) without adult evaluative intervention

Materials

Pieces of carpet, rags, cardboards, or old socks (see "Carpet Skates" in "Making Equipment at Little or No Cost")

Directions

Have each child place a piece of carpet (or rag, etc.) under each foot. To move, a participant must ski, slide, or skate.

Comments and Suggestions
- For skiing a carpet strip or rag should be big enough so that the player's whole foot can be placed upon it.

- Old socks can be used under or even on the feet.
- Mat backing on rugs seems to hold up better than rubberized backing.
- The size of the carpet should be changed to meet the needs of your group.
- Cut carpets frequently shed. We usually have the children play a clean-up game after using carpets.
- Pieces of cardboard sometimes work well on carpeted floors.
- Skiing and skating seem to allow for a great deal of vigorous activity in a small space and reduce injuries from impact force.
- The development of the abdominal muscles is very important, since it contributes to the improvement of balance and trunk control that can allow a child to move more successfully and with less risk of injury in all movement activities.
- Placing children who are not disabled on carpets can help equalize the group when a disabled child does not use carpets. This should always be the choice of the disabled child. If he or she also wants to use the carpets, let him or her do so.
- This activity can allow a child to discover how to do something while struggling with a difficult challenge. This struggle and the accompanying self-evaluation, perseverance, and improvement is empowering to a child, fostering an "I can!" attitude. Because this process may involve a period of fumbling (discovering), adults may want to help the children to find the answer(s). This can reduce the opportunity for the children to experience their ability to overcome a difficult challenge. Our task is to engineer the environment so that the children can experience this discovery process. You may want to consider sending this activity home as a parent involvement opportunity, along with information on making carpet skates.

Simplifications and Challenges

- Carpet activities can be applied to each of the following games:

Cross Over	Robot
Squirrels in the Trees	Washing Machine (below)
Freeze	Car and Driver
Help!	Busy Bee and Back to Back
The Winds Are Changing	Farmer-Farmer
Rise and Shine	

- "Washing Machine"—A whole story about washing clothes can be acted out, including hanging up the clothes to dry and then having the clothes blow in the wind.

Thanks to Jack Brenner and Rick Cawley for the suggestion of using pieces of cardboard.

The "Washing Machine" variation came from Maryanne Tobin.

clapping words ^(H)

Life Skills
- Increasing attention span and concentration
- Developing auditory figure and ground discrimination—selective listening
- Analyzing situations
- Finding similarities and differences
- Recognizing patterns
- Creating a specific pattern of sound
- Developing individual involvement and commitment to a response
- Developing personal identity with others within a group
- Practicing evaluation and critical thinking
- Developing an awareness of syllabic division, which is important in developing listening skills and spelling and linguistic development

Materials   No special materials are needed.

Directions   The leader begins by saying a familiar word and clapping the syllables at the same time. The children respond by repeating the word accompanied by the appropriate number of claps.

Comments and Suggestions
- In the beginning, say the word slowly and enunciate very clearly.
- Some players may need help. Try to observe closely those who seem hesitant or inconsistent. Feel free to move among the group during the game.
- You may discover a participant who needs a hearing examination. Players who have difficulty dividing words into syllables may not be

hearing part of the word. A participant may have learned to cope with this limitation to some degree by using whatever pieces of a word can be heard to guess at the meaning. The problem may sometimes mask itself by making a participant seem inattentive and slow.

- Playing this game may be a good way for the group to learn a new child's name.
- Playing this game may help participants to learn hard-to-pronounce and unfamiliar names and words.
- Playing this game may help children who speak English as a second language.
- You may eventually want to allow the children to suggest words to use.

Simplifications and Challenges

- Use various words based on a theme, such as seasonal words, months of the year, pieces of furniture, colors, and foods.
- Have the children take turns choosing words.
- Have the children take turns finding a picture or an object in the room to use.
- Have the children use this activity to review what they saw on a field trip, to reinforce new vocabulary words, or to increase memory.
- Use the children's last names.
- Use the children's birth months.
- Have children learn to clap the syllables of their first name and then move around to try to find those who have the same number of syllables in their names.
- Rather than clapping, have the children march in place to get their whole bodies into the syllabic rhythm.

© Addison-Wesley Publishing Company, Inc.

cows and ducks

Life Skills
- Making decisions
- Focusing attention and concentrating
- Developing auditory discrimination and an awareness from which direction a sound originates; these life skills are vital for learning, safety, and enjoyment
- Developing spatial awareness (an awareness of space, relative distance, and relationships within space)
- Developing auditory figure and ground discrimination (the ability to separate and select a given relevant auditory stimulus from competing irrelevant background sounds)
- Getting the idea

Materials
No special materials are needed.

Directions
Whisper either "cow" or "duck" in each child's ear. All children begin making the appropriate sound of their animal. Similar animals try to find each other. Have the children who have found the other cows and ducks continue to make their sounds. This continues their level of involvement and should give additional louder and clearer auditory input for the children who need it.

Comments and Suggestions
- If the basic game is too complicated for your children, break the activity into parts. The parts can then be added together gradually over time as the children can handle a new challenge.

- Have the children all make the sound of a cow or a duck. Perhaps you could hold up a picture or drawing and they could respond with the appropriate sound.
- Make the sound of a duck and have all the children respond by going to a part of the room designated as a pond. Moo like a cow and have all move to a part of the room that is the barn.
- Distribute a cow or duck card to each child. Children look at the picture on the card and make the appropriate sound. They then attempt to find all the other children making the same sound. The children can check their cards with each other after the groups are formed. The cards are collected, shuffled, and redistributed to the children to play again.
- Build a progression that would develop over time. Repeating a game several times over a period of time allows the children to get the idea and may also allow for children to help each other.

Simplifications and Challenges

- Using baby chicks and kittens can inspire a quiet version of the game.
- Children may eventually be able to choose which animal they want to be, begin making the sound, and form groups without being assigned ahead of time.

cross over

Life Skills
- Focusing attention
- "Reading one's environment" through spatial awareness (an awareness of space, relative distance, and relationships within space); interpreting multiple stimuli; adapting to a changing environment and attempting to respond appropriately
- Developing kinesthetic awareness (ability to perceive one's body positions from sensory messages received from end organs located in the muscles, tendons, and joints)
- Generating alternatives
- Making decisions
- Practicing self-evaluation
- Being responsible for one's own and others' safety

Materials
No special materials are needed.

Directions
Players form two lines facing each other about 10 feet apart. On a signal all players must try to cross to the other side without touching one another. Challenge the children to do this very carefully. This is an excellent preliminary to many other activities that involve an awareness of space and moving in relation to others. After the first few crossings, you may want to ask if anyone noticed how someone else successfully accomplished the task. Volunteers are asked to identify the person they saw, describe what the person did, and explain why it was successful. This approach encourages generating alternatives to problems, involvement, learning from each other, cooperative learning, and group bonding.

© Addison-Wesley Publishing Company, Inc.

Comments and Suggestions

- Add simple body positions, such as hands on heads, hands on hips, arms at sides, arms straight out. This allows the children to discover early on that changes may require adaptations in relation to personal space. Elimination is not necessary in such activities. The challenge is sufficient, and the child who might be eliminated is frequently the one who needs the involvement the most.
- If participants intentionally bump each other you may want to move to activities that help to reduce this type of behavior, such as "Help!", "Robot," "Car and Driver," "Islands," and "Mirroring." If these players only want more action, attempt to raise their challenge level by having them skip, hop, or tip-toe. Some challenges (skip, hop) increase the task difficulty. If the bumping is accidental, tip-toe or slow motion will decrease bumping without increasing the skill level.
- A wonderfully positive way to deal with bumping is to have players who make contact freeze; unfreeze the players with a light tap or gesture.
- Remind players of their "Cross Over" skills when they are involved in other activities.

Simplifications and Challenges

- Have adults model crossing over without touching. Then call on just two children to play. Increase the number of children who are called to cross over until all are crossing at once or until the space limits or ability levels are reached.
- Have players try to move in slow motion. This variation may be helpful when you have only a small space in which to play, and it also gives the needed time to increase body space and kinesthetic awareness (ability to perceive one's body positions from sensory messages received from end organs located in the muscles, tendons, and joints).
- Have partners cross over holding hands or hooking elbows.
- Have players form a circle.

- Have the children attempt to balance a napkin on their head as they move across the area.
- Have children wear carpet skates (see page 73).
- Teach "Cross Over." Then play "Cross Over," focusing on spatial awareness (an awareness of space, relative distance, and relationships within space) by having the children walk all around the room. When you say "spaghetti line," all the children must join hands with those near them to form a long line. In later experiences with spaghetti lines, have children try to form one long line with everyone joining hands.
- Suggest different types of movement: walk backward, spin, hop, jump.

Thanks to Jodi Whitmoyer for suggesting a positive way to handle bumping problems. She calls the teacher's tap a "kiss from a butterfly."

farmer-farmer

Life Skills
- Developing spatial awareness (an awareness of space, relative distance, and relationships within space)
- Estimating distance and speed
- Increasing attention span and concentration
- Developing anticipation and prediction
- Practicing self-control within a state of excitement
- Taking responsibility for others (not bumping)
- Choosing a level of risk taking
- Assessing a situation and responding effectively when excited
- Increasing body control and agility

Materials   No special materials are needed.

Directions   The leader, "Farmer-Farmer," pretends to be looking for something. The players either follow or circle "Farmer-Farmer," saying the following lines.

Players: Farmer-Farmer, what are you looking for?

Farmer-Farmer: Some string.

Players: What do you need a string for?

Farmer-Farmer: To mend my basket.

Players: What do you need a basket for?

Farmer-Farmer: To gather peaches.

At this last statement, two or more children can join hands or a child can place both hands on top of his or her head; these actions make the children invisible, so that they cannot be caught (put into the basket as

83

peaches). Children who are caught join the farmer and the game starts over. Young players seem to enjoy the repetition and stimulation of this game. It may be that they enjoy the excitement and "danger" of being caught when the timing and outcome can be predictable and somewhat within their control.

Comments and Suggestions

- You may wish to teach the players the repeated words and/or tell a story prior to the activity.
- You may want to remain in the role of Farmer-Farmer until the players are ready to lead.
- Remind children to be careful not to run into others as they play.
- Each participant may play as near to or as far from Farmer-Farmer as he or she chooses. Thus children can individually determine how ready they are to take a risk and how much of a risk they are willing to take.
- You may want to create boundaries for this game so that children do not run into walls and other obstacles.
- If children need extra practice at self-control, they could play "Cross Over" as a warm-up activity.

Simplifications and Challenges

- Vary the actions that prevent children from getting caught. For example, children could be required to freeze on one foot, sit down in a designated area, put their hands on their knees, and so on.
- You may soon discover that children want to get caught, which diminishes participation. To avoid this problem, simply choose a new Farmer-Farmer's helper for each round.
- Change the theme of Farmer-Farmer to reflect the needs or interests of your children. For example, seasonal themes could be incorporated by having a turkey, Jack Frost, or a leprechaun lead the game.

Thanks to Susan Blackaby for this revision of the Giant-Giant game.

find it

Life Skills
- Reinforcing learned information
- Becoming more aware of one's environment
- Sharing space, cooperating, being responsible not to bump into others, spatial awareness (an awareness of space, relative distance, and relationships within space)
- Solving problems; making choices

Materials
- Colored pieces of construction paper (optional)

Directions

Call out a color to players as they move around the room. Players must then locate something that color and touch it. All should try to find ways to help each other touch the color, either directly or indirectly. For example, to form a spaghetti connection, the first person to reach a particular color extends a hand to take the next person's hand and so on and so on until all have joined. This type of activity may increase group bonding while supporting increased trust, autonomy, and initiative. Encouragement could come from a statement such as, "Our job isn't done until we are all connected."

Comments and Suggestions
- Depending upon space and abilities, players may need to *walk* to the color called.
- Encourage children to locate more than one example of the color.
- You may want to play "Islands" beforehand to help the players learn to share.

Simplifications and Challenges

- The activity could be made more personal by adding a favorite color call.
- Use other concepts: numbers, letters, shapes.
- The players must touch and remain in touch with a particular color, shape, number, or letter until the next signal is given.
- The players could touch or hold the hand of anyone wearing a called color. Others could then hold a free hand of a connected participant.
- You could ask questions that are answered by colors ("What color is the sky?") and have children respond by finding the color.

follow me [H]

Life Skills
- Developing focus, attention, and concentration
- Careful reading of one's environment
- Seeing and reproducing specific movements accurately (this allows one to learn motor skills much more rapidly)
- Learning that perseverance leads to improvement and increased success

Materials

No special materials are needed.

Directions

The leader stands facing the group and extends arms in a very specific (held) position. The players are asked to duplicate this position. When all are in position, the leader assumes a new pose.

Comments and Suggestions

- Simple patterns are those in which the arms are in similar positions (both arms straight out, both arms up) or both hands are placed on the same body part (hands on hips, hands on head). You may wish to begin with these simple patterns and then add complexity as the year goes on by placing your arms in a bent position, having each arm in a different position, or involving more body parts. You are seeking growth in each child's awareness of specifics within the environment. Challenge all your children by allowing them to enter at their own present level of ability and do the best they can to attempt to duplicate what they see. Awareness and improvement will come with practice and self-correction.

- After each move to a new position, allow time for everyone to participate. A pause allows children to process information at their own pace or level. Rushing to the next movement or increasing your body tension can contribute to the excitement and the challenge, but pausing after reaching the new position allows all to complete the important process. Rushing on too soon to the next position can leave some children frustrated if they have not had the opportunity to mentally process and respond. Reading one's environment is a very important perceptual motor process and life skill that requires perceiving, mentally processing the information, making a motor response or commitment, and having some time and opportunity to evaluate feedback. Learning how to challenge all your children through this process of rush and pause is acquired through awareness and practice.

- This activity can be used to get children's attention and as a quickie. Start with a very obvious position and continue until one child after another notices and joins in, enabling you to move more easily to a new activity or task.
- When the children have become familiar with this activity and have a repertoire of moves from their experience with this game, you might periodically ask for a volunteer to help lead it.

Simplifications and Challenges

- Offer this activity as a series of challenges. The challenge does not have to be spoken. The attitude or words "Can you do this one?" may create a sense of challenge and reduce the temporary frustration of initial failure.
- Repeat the same motion 3–5 times in a row. Then have the children attempt to do the motion the number of times it was done. This may work well for the young child, since it builds in a natural pause to get the idea before having to begin the motion. It also allows for children of varying levels of ability to feel challenged at their level (equalization).
- Motion stories can be incorporated and later lead to "Bear or Lion Hunt."

- A year-long memory challenge might be to have children take the position that you have just done as you move on to the next position.
- A related activity, very much like "Follow Me," is "Wind, Rain, and Thunder," page 150.

Thanks to Earle Matlack for the suggestion of using "Follow Me" as an attention-getter.

freeze [H]

Life Skills
- Practicing body control (balance; ability to stop, start, and hold one's position)
- Developing kinesthetic awareness (ability to perceive one's body positions from sensory messages received from end organs located in the muscles, tendons, and joints)
- Developing body and space relationships (estimation and relationships in space)
- Increasing attention span and concentration (need to remain alert)
- Practicing self-evaluation

Materials
No special materials are needed.

Directions
The players begin to move, slowly at first. They are encouraged to increase the activity and type of movements they are using. At the signal "freeze," all players stop. They try to stay still and hold the frozen position until "melt" is called.

Comments and Suggestions
- Body control and balance are important skills. All movement is based upon these, and many serious accidents can be avoided once children have developed these abilities.
- The signal to "freeze" can be used at other times when you wish the group to stop all action.
- This activity can also be done sitting, standing, or lying down.
- You may need to help children understand the concept of "freeze." Play "Follow Me" and stop suddenly. As the children follow this quick

90

© Addison-Wesley Publishing Company, Inc.

stop motion, say "freeze." This conceptualization can then be transferred to the game of "Freeze."

Simplifications and Challenges

- This activity can be done in slow motion. Players challenge themselves with a variety of moves.
- Play music, as in "Islands." When the music stops, the players freeze. Melt occurs when the music begins again.
- You could add a challenge for any participant who wishes to accept it. For example, "Can you hold your position with one eye closed?"
- Add music and play "Dance and Freeze."
- Encourage children to be creative by going from one expressive pose and hold to another whenever you give a signal. Little space is needed for this form of the activity.

Thanks to Mary Felix and Sally Henry for the suggestion of using "Follow Me" to get across the concept of "freeze."

going on a trip (H)

Life Skills
- Developing memory skills
- Developing listening skills and audiovisual relationships
- Focusing concentration and increasing attention span
- Practicing duplication of movement
- Practicing self-evaluation
- Handling stress in a safe environment
- Sharing, contributing, leading, following

Materials
No special materials are needed.

Directions
Every participant is asked to select some motion or movement to share with the group. Ask for volunteers, giving some players time to think and providing examples for those who may not have any immediate ideas. A circle is formed, and the trip begins: "I am [name]. I am going on a trip. I am going to take [name of article and motion] on our trip." The whole group then says "This is [name]. [Name] is going to take [name of article] on our trip." All players who can remember do the motion as they say this.

The next volunteer says: "I am [name] and I am going on the trip, too. I am going to take [article and motion]." The first volunteer now raises his or her hand and all who remember say in unison, "This is [name]. [name] is going to take [article and motion].

Players then repeat the name, article, and motion of the second volunteer, and a third volunteer is added. Each volunteer adds a name and a motion, and the procedure continues, reiterating each volunteer's

© Addison-Wesley Publishing Company, Inc.

name, article, and motion before adding a new one. If the group seems to be inattentive the leader may choose to place a hand over a player's head and ask the group to respond by identifying that person's name, article, and motion.

If you have a large group, you may want to do only a few motions each day. Doing only a few each day tests long-term memory and may also give some players an opportunity to think about what they would like to do. With a large group this is also helpful in avoiding boredom when an activity becomes too long and drawn out.

Comments and Suggestions

- This activity is helpful when a new participant enters the group.
- This activity helps everyone learn or review names.
- Verbalizing can be difficult for many preschoolers. This activity may allow children to work on this together in a safe environment. It is important that we continue to select and modify activities in order to increase social and emotional as well as physical safety factors.
- Using volunteers avoids unnecessary tension for a player who does not have a motion yet or is still getting the idea of the game.
- Notice that the group response in this game allows all to test their memory, takes the focus off failure, and allows each player to participate at his or her level. You can analyze expansion (increasing the number of turns or opportunities to participate in an important developmental experience); equalization (giving each player an opportunity to participate at her or his level of ability); and interactive challenge (equalization that allows participants who vary in abilities to be able to interact and contribute reciprocally to each other's growth process) as this activity is played.

Simplifications and Challenges

- If the class has been on a walk or trip together, let children name several objects, animals, or people that they saw. Then ask the group if they can all act out the objects that have been named. Ask for volunteers to show their favorites. The motions shown become the motions for the game.

- One teacher, Sherry McBride, uses this game to help children learn each other's names. She sits her children in a circle. She tells her group that they are going on an imaginary trip (through the forest, up a mountain, etc.) "The road is very narrow so we'll have to follow one another. I'll be the leader, since I have taken this trip before. My name is Ms. McBride. I am going up the mountain and Michael (child next in circle) will follow me."

  Children say, "Michael will follow Ms. McBride. Ms. McBride knows the way."

  Michael then says, "My name is Michael. I am going up the mountain behind Ms. McBride. Tina (the child next in the circle) will follow me."

  Children say, "Tina will follow Michael, Michael will follow Ms. McBride. Ms. McBride knows the way."

© Addison-Wesley Publishing Company, Inc.

help!

Life Skills
- Helping others and being helped by others
- Solving problems
- Making decisions
- Developing spatial awareness (an awareness of space, relative distance, and relationships within space)
- Practicing balance
- Practicing self-evaluation

Materials
- Paper napkins or tissues

Directions
The object of this activity is to move around in the available space while carrying a paper napkin on one's head, avoiding any object or other individual. If the paper falls, a player is frozen. Another player can assist the frozen player by recovering the dropped napkin and replacing it on the head of the frozen player. If replacing a napkin that has dropped to the floor is too difficult for young players, have the helper merely touch a frozen player to unfreeze her or him. This player then replaces her or his own napkin. The choice of which type of help to give could be left up to the individual helper, allowing each child to make this decision.

Comments and Suggestions
- If there is only a limited amount of space available, you may want to emphasize moving in slow motion.
- Sometimes music is nice; "Help" by the Beatles might be fun.
- Any piece of paper can be used. We have found that napkins, toilet paper, and tissues are usually available and can be made larger or

95

smaller to accommodate various levels of ability. You may want to leave the choice of level of difficulty up to each player.

- You may want to have your children practice saying "thank you" and "you're welcome" as they help each other.
- The players could play "Cross Over" and/or "Carpet Skiing" before this activity, so that they have developed the ability to avoid bumping into each other.

Simplifications and Challenges

- You may want to start by having players replace their own napkins when they fall. Build up to having a child freeze if the napkin falls; you unfreeze the child with a gentle touch. Later the other children can help the frozen children.
- This activity could be done wearing carpet skates (see page 73).

Thanks to Phil Gerney for introducing us to this activity.
The idea of using music was Lois Klevan's, as was the idea of letting a helper merely touch a frozen player to unfreeze her or him.

© Addison-Wesley Publishing Company, Inc.

I am a balloon ^(H)

Life Skills
- Making personal choices, the beginning of independence, initiative
- Releasing tension and excessive energy through deep breathing

Materials
- A balloon (optional)

Directions

Ask that all players shake loose and collapse as much as possible. Say something like: "You are a great saggy balloon and you have no air in you. Can you go absolutely limp? Now when you hear this sound— *shhhh*, you will know that you are being slowly filled with air. Some of you will fill all over while others may fill only one arm or leg at a time. Let's try it. *Shhhh...sh...sh...sh...shhhhhh.*"

Take your time and allow the players to really work at becoming slowly filled with air. Then you might say: "Now you are getting just about as full as you can. *Shhhhh....* Are your lungs filled? Are you as big as you can possibly be? Oh! You have developed a slow leak! *Ssss....* Are you beginning to droop?

"*Sssssssssssss... sssssss... sss....* Are you just about collapsed? Do you feel yourself totally collapsed and limp? Is your head heavy? Are your arms and legs completely relaxed? Is your body sinking into the floor [or your chair]? Hey, they put a patch on you. Now they're going to put air in you again." Continue from there.

Comments and Suggestions
- Having a balloon on hand might be fun.
- This activity can be done sitting or standing.
- You might walk around and lift an arm here or there to see if a participant can really go limp. Some cannot and may need to

participate in other activities that can help them learn to relax, such as "Old MacDonald Had a Body," "Jell-O Jiggle," "Rise and Shine," "Letting Go," and "Farmer-Farmer." We have also found that as children feel comfortable within a group or there is an increase in their self-esteem, they are able to relax more.

- This activity has been used to calm excited players and relax tense, nervous ones.

Simplifications and Challenges

- If there is plenty of room, blow up a balloon and let it go. It will normally shoot all over the room, and the players can simulate this action. Be sure they are aware of their "no bumping" responsibility. ("Cross Over" might be a good preliminary activity.) You can also have the players be small balloons that get popped by a pin, collapsing and relaxing quickly.
- You could tell a story about a weather balloon caught in gusts of wind, hit by rain drops, floating gently in the sunshine, and so on, and have children act out the scenario.
- To start this activity you may wish to have a whole group balloon, having all players hold hands.

Thanks to Jamie Huntley and Karen Hammer for the whole group balloon suggestion.

islands

Life Skills
- Developing simple auditory awareness and alert listening
- Practicing body and space relationships
- Practicing motor planning
- Practicing space estimation
- Making decisions
- Practicing self-control and cooperation
- Developing sense of unity
- Solving problems: developing the ability to choose, see alternatives, change one's mind, and work with others

Materials
- A source of music or sound (or use clapping)
- Islands made of large pieces of butcher paper, plastic hoops, rugs, large towels, or other material that children can safely step and stand on without slipping

Directions

Players move among the islands. When the music or leader's clapping stops, all players find an island. Sharing an island with others is fine.

Comments and Suggestions
- Turning the volume control up and down is an alternative to turning the music source on and off.
- As the children seem ready to accept a new challenge you might ask "Can you try to find a different island each time?"
- Later, children can be further challenged by having an island removed and trying to get on the remaining islands.
- As the children can handle fewer islands, you might want to remove even more and see if all the children can fit on the remaining islands.

The basic concept in cooperation is for all involved to overcome a common problem or to obtain a difficult goal. When everyone is able to be on the remaining islands, everyone is a winner.

- This may be a nice time to take pictures for the bulletin board. A title could be "Working together WE can make it work."
- If you wish to make your own plastic hoops, see page 164 in "Making Equipment at Little or No Cost."
- Suggest that parents use "Islands" as an alternative to "Musical Chairs" for children's parties.

Simplifications and Challenges

- For young children, you may create islands of different colors. Then ask *all* the children to move to the green island, for example, and challenge them to try to get everyone on that one. Numbers or shapes can also be used. At a higher level, the children could be asked to move to the island on which the number is less than 3 or more than 3, and so on. The children work together to try to solve the problems.

Thanks to Randi Heller for the suggestion of using different colors for the islands.

© Addison-Wesley Publishing Company, Inc.

jell-o® jiggle (H)

Life Skills
- Developing body awareness
- Practicing conscious control of an isolated body part
- Learning to be able to relax and control tension buildup
- Developing knowledge of body parts

Materials
- Music (optional)

Directions

Ask the players: "Have you ever seen a bowl of Jell-O (gelatin dessert) jiggle? Have you ever opened the refrigerator and seen it wiggle: It doesn't move like anything else in the whole world. Jam doesn't move that way, and worms don't wiggle that way. It is very special. Can you move like Jell-O? Can you let your shoulders jiggle like Jell-O? While you are jiggling your arms and shoulders, can you start your hips moving? Can you be loose in the knees? Can you wobble very, very slowly until you are in slow motion? Can you wobble forward and backward? Can you wobble in a circle? Can you wobble the other direction in a circle? Can your wobble include some up and down motions? Do you feel loose? Can you wiggle with a friend? Perhaps we could make up a new dance and call it the 'Jell-O Jiggle.' Do you think we could put it to music?"

Comments and Suggestions
- It seems that when tension and stress are reduced, self-control increases or becomes easier.
- Make up a story to go with the motions, or perhaps let the players try.
- "Can You?" questioning and involvement may improve players' general attention span and concentration and promote better listening skills.

101

- It might be fun to make gelatin dessert in conjunction with this activity.
- Pace is an important aspect of exploring movement. Allow enough time for players to try each motion.
- Remember that there are no right and wrong answers in this type of activity. The attempt is the important aspect.
- This activity seems to work well at the end of an active day.
- You might want to have the children pretend or fantasize that they are very carefully carrying a bowl of Jell-O.
- If the players seem hesitant, shy, or distracted by others, you might consider having them do the activity with their eyes closed.

Simplifications and Challenges

- Have children play the Hokey Pokey.
- The activity can be done lying on floor.
- Make this into a group activity by having players all join hands.
- Use the activity to play "The Factory": "Hello. I work in a factory. I have a cat and a dog and a family. One day my boss came up to me and said 'Are you busy?' I said, 'No.' He said, 'Then turn the knob with your right hand.'" Repeat the story in a sing-song fashion, adding left hand, right foot, left foot, back side, then head. At the end when the boss says, "Are you busy?" the answer is YES!

Thanks to Patricia Isabella for the suggestion of having the players join hands.

Jell-O is a registered trademark of Kraft General Foods, Inc.

© Addison-Wesley Publishing Company, Inc.

letting go ^(H)

Life Skills
- Isolating and controlling specific body segments
- Becoming more aware of one's physical state of tension
- Increasing one's attention span and ability to concentrate
- Increasing neuromuscular relaxation (control of physical reactions to stress); conscious control over muscular tension and relaxation
- Developing thinking processes, mind-body interaction

Materials
No special materials are needed.

Directions
Players learn to relax and be in control of their body tensions by participating in activities that make them aware of these factors. Players pretend to be a wind-up toy that gradually runs down, a melting ice cube or chocolate, a puppet, a rag doll, a tire going slowly flat. Also play "Tense and Relax": While players lie on the floor, ask them to tense a particular body part, stretch the part as much as they can, and then relax.

Comments and Suggestions
- Try to allow time for total relaxation. It will take some children longer than others, but these are probably the children who need this experience most. Repetition and practice over time allow players to become skillful.
- See "Rise and Shine," "I Am a Balloon," "Jell-O Jiggle," and "Old Mac-Donald Had a Body" for other activities that help children learn to relax.
- Extend this activity by making up a story to go with the motions or mood.

- Music sometimes helps set the tone for this activity.
- In a stress-producing world it has become important that people learn to relax at as early an age as possible.
- The detrimental effects of tension are being seen in increasing numbers of young children.

living basketball ^(H)

Life Skills
- Throwing accuracy, especially follow through
- Developing spatial awareness (an awareness of space, relative distance, and relationships within space)
- Developing depth perception
- Judging distance
- Practicing object manipulation
- Solving problems
- Making decisions
- Practicing self-evaluation
- Practicing evaluation and adaptation
- Persevering
- Learning that through effort you can improve
- Accepting responsibility, helping others succeed, cooperating

Materials
- Soft trash balls (see "Making Equipment at Little or no Cost," page 160)
- Large bags or boxes

Directions

In this cooperative activity, everyone wins. Groups can be of 2–5 members, but the smaller the team, the more turns each player gets. One or two players hold open a large bag. Other players shoot trash balls and try to sink them in the bag. Each player can have three or four balls; players can make their own equipment. Bag holders and shooters can both participate in making a goal. The bag holders can move the bag to help catch the trash balls.

Comments and Suggestions

- Soft objects are necessary to avoid injury to the bag holder.
- Some teachers prefer not to use plastic bags with young children due to the safety factor.
- At first you may want to ask more experienced players to be the bag holders, or you may want to ask for volunteers to help in providing children with a leadership opportunity (taking the initiative).
- Less experienced players may need to stand closer to the bag. This choice should be available to everyone. The adult in charge should clarify that the choice is available without making the choice for a child.

Simplifications and Challenges

- See "Newspaper Delivery."

106

magic jumping beans ^(H)

Life Skills
- Increasing attention span and concentration
- Practicing self-control in a state of excitement

Materials   No special materials are needed.

Directions   Encourage children to act out the following story: "When I was a small child my mother and father gave me these wonderful magic jumping beans. Does anyone know what jumping beans do? Can you all wiggle and move like my magical jumping beans did?

"While my mother and father were with me the beans would wiggle and move like you are doing. At night I put the beans carefully away. The next morning I took out my magical jumping beans. They did not move. They just lay there quietly.

"As I turned my back on the jumping beans to go get my mother and father [turn your back deliberately and slowly] I thought the beans began to move just a little. [At least one or two children may get the idea and wiggle or move a little. Turn back to face children, acting surprised.]

"Did any of you see any of the jumping beans move when I wasn't looking?" [Slowly turn your back on the children again. If you begin to hear giggles you can assume the children are beginning to get the idea. Pretend you are trying to catch the children moving as you turn to go get help. Children seem to love the excitement of trying to fool the leader. To end the activity you can pretend to put the jumping beans away.] "Perhaps we'll check out those jumping beans again another day."

Comments and Suggestions

- "Freeze" might be a good preliminary activity.
- This might be a good preliminary activity for "Farmer-Farmer."

Simplifications and Challenges

- If you feel your children have enough self-control, have them stand to play the game.

Thanks to Paula Malek for sharing this game with us.

108

meetball(H)

Life Skills
- Developing social responsibility and sharing
- Practicing group bonding
- Developing memory skills
- Throwing and catching (or rolling/sliding and receiving)
- Learning and remembering people's names

Materials
- A yarn ball or other soft object for each group

Directions

In a circle formation, a SOFT object such as a yarn ball is tossed, slid, or rolled from player to player. This could also be a small pillow or a large, loosely packed wad of paper covered with a plastic bag. Each player says his or her name as he or she receives the object until you feel that the players are beginning to remember names. At that point you may want to initiate a "group shout," in which all players call out the receiver's name. Players are encouraged to remember as many names as possible. Be sure to note the modification in Simplifications and Challenges.

Comments and Suggestions

- Beginning by having players sit and slide the object may help maintain control while the children get the idea of how the game is played.
- The use of a yarn ball rather than a regular ball is important because it is less apt to separate the skilled from the less skilled players when catching is involved. A yarn ball may also help reduce the fear some players have of an oncoming object, and it allows the game to be played safely almost anywhere. The group should be encouraged to include all players if this does not occur automatically. Ask, "Can those

of you with good memories help us to remember who still needs to receive the ball?" This is a good activity to help a teacher or leader learn the names of group members or to help a new child feel more comfortable in a new situation.

- If you have help you may want to break your group into smaller groups to increase individual involvement and make it easier to learn names. You may want to consider changing the groups to increase the challenge and number of names being learned.

- Even though you are encouraging total inclusion, a player should still be allowed to pass to whomever he or she wishes, which gives the uncertain participant a degree of comfort.

- A bean bag in a plastic bag will slide on carpeting.

Simplifications and Challenges

- Slide a block, bean bag, or eraser a short distance to each child. The child says his or her name and slides the object back to you. If a child doesn't respond, say the child's name and ask him or her to slide the object back to you. Have a second object ready and simply go on to another child if there is still no response. After playing this several times, say, "I think this is a silly game. When the block comes to you we'll all call your name." This will involve the children in a group shout.

Thanks to Sherry McBride for the "silly game" variation and rhyme.

110

© Addison-Wesley Publishing Company, Inc.

memory teaser [H]

Life Skills
- Sequencing
- Developing short-term memory skills
- Practicing self-evaluation

Materials   No special materials are needed.

Directions   Challenge the children to remember three things sequentially. For example, "Can you stand up, turn around, and sit down?" Build toward more difficult sequences such as, "Can you march ten times in place, jump ten times, and then clap ten times?"

Comments and Suggestions
- Start at the children's ability level and gradually increase the degree of difficulty and challenge.

mirroring ^(H)

Life Skills
- Developing visual alertness
- Developing visual sensitivity to change
- Monitoring the details of one's environment; noticing change and responding appropriately
- Developing spatial awareness (an awareness of space, relative distance, and relationships within space)
- Developing focus, attention, and concentration
- Persevering

Materials
- Music (optional)

Directions

Face the group and move in a slow, continuous motion that the players duplicate as if they are looking into a mirror.

Comments and Suggestions
- You might want to lead up to this activity by simply having the children do slow-motion movements. The challenge is to see how slowly they can move.
- If players have difficulty with "Mirroring," consider "Follow Me" or "Can You?"
- If you are playing with a very young child you may want to start by mirroring her or his movements.
- As this activity becomes familiar, some children may be able to take turns leading the group. This is easier if the children have had previous experience in leading "Follow Me."

112

Simplifications and Challenges

- Go from simple (only one body part moving) to complex (more than one body part moving at the same time).
- Have the players do the activity while sitting.
- Combine the activity with "Streamers."
- After the children are really comfortable with this activity they might try working with partners, facing each other and standing relatively close together. One participant begins moving slowly and the other follows. After a period of experimentation, partners change roles. The use of slow background music might help keep partners moving slowly at first.

newspaper delivery

Life Skills
- Throwing for accuracy, learning to follow through
- Throwing for force if distance is increased
- Making estimations
- Functioning with a purpose
- Practicing self-evaluation
- Functioning without constant adult supervision
- Persevering

Materials
- Several newspapers folded to be approximately 4 inches wide, soft enough to absorb force when the newspaper hits the wall; fasten them with rubberbands
- A large box to catch newspapers that fall after hitting the wall
- A large plain drawing of a house

Directions

A drawing of a house is attached to a wall, allowing plenty of space for throwing. This drawing should be placed above a large box. As a newspaper is tossed against the wall it will fall into the box, acting both as a receptacle for the tossed papers and as a means of evaluating the success of the throw.

Children choose the distance from which to throw the newspapers at the drawing of the house. This encourages the children to make as many choices as possible at their level of decision-making ability. Engineer the environment to foster this process while also making the situation safe socially, emotionally, and physically for all involved.

After completing a turn, a child may take another turn unless

© Addison-Wesley Publishing Company, Inc.

someone is waiting. If you find that your children enjoy this activity, you may want to set up more than one house or encourage parents to set up the activity at home.

Comments and Suggestions

- Children will seek growth and competency in activities that are meaningful to them.
- The choice of short throwing distances will help the child develop accuracy and reinforce a sense of success; choosing longer distances will support the development of force abilities and will allow the child to risk success. We believe that the child will choose most wisely for him- or herself.
- If the newspaper leaves undesired marks on the wall, each paper can be wrapped in a plastic bag or a sheet can be used (see note below).
- If noise, force damage, space, or newspaper marks are concerns, you may want to hang a large cloth sheet (house can be drawn on this) away from the wall and allow it to be used as a target. You may need a deeper or larger box since the force of the throw will carry the sheet backward and the newspapers will drop accordingly.

Simplifications and Challenges

- This might be a good preliminary activity for "Living Basketball."

old macdonald had a body (H)

Life Skills
- Learning to get rid of body tensions
- Learning to participate in a group while making an individual contribution
- Developing anticipation and prediction
- Developing auditory alertness

Materials

No special materials are needed.

Directions

"Old MacDonald Had a Farm" becomes a stretching song: "Old MacDonald had a body, E-I-E-I-O. And on this body he had two arms, E-I-E-I-O. With a stretch, stretch here, and a stretch, stretch there, and here a stretch, there a stretch, everywhere a stretch, stretch, Old MacDonald had a body, E-I-E-I-O."

Alternate song lyrics to the same tune could be: "I can stretch from head to toe, E-I-E-I-O. (children stretching) I can stretch my _____ just so, E-I-E-I-O. With a stretch, stretch here," (and so on).

Comments and Suggestions
- This activity can be done sitting or standing.
- You may start this activity by having the children call out a body part and point to it. Move quickly behind each child and ask the group if they can stretch (wiggle, shake, twist) the body part this child is pointing to. This warm-up provides children with suggestions to draw from until the children have gotten the idea of what they are to do.

116

- After the players understand the basic pattern, they can select the body parts to be stretched.
- This activity can be used with participants who are learning to identify body parts.
- Remember, restless players are trying to limit their movement. They need an exercise such as this one, periodically, to express their need to move.

Simplifications and Challenges

- Shaking, twisting, wiggling can be substituted for stretching.

Thanks to Susan Blackaby for the alternate song lyrics.

parts and points(H)

Life Skills
- Reinforcing body part locations
- Listening
- Following verbal instructions
- Increasing attention span and concentration
- Developing auditory focus
- Accepting a challenge
- Making decisions

Materials

No special materials are needed.

Directions

Challenge all the players by asking them to show you the location of various body parts (ears, feet, shoulders, etc.) on their bodies.

Comments and Suggestions
- This activity has been used to calm players when they have just come from an experience that encouraged hyperactivity and there is a need to reduce their excitement level.
- Speaking very softly as you give the challenges also helps to create a quieter and more relaxed atmosphere.
- This activity could be used as a quick break.
- This game can be played sitting as well as standing.

Simplifications and Challenges
- Use body "points" such as elbow, nose, knee, and so on. You may need to check whether players understand "point" and can identify where some "points" are on the body.
- Ask the players if they can try to close their eyes and locate body parts or points. At first you may find that some children will need to keep

their eyes open all or part of the time, but try to observe these children over several sessions to see their progress. Remember that children will do something when they can. These games make "challenges to grow on" and allow each child to buy in when ready. *Follow Me Too* games allow for this. Make the challenge clear, but also be patient.

- Children may also enjoy "Touch your fingers with your friend's fingers" or "Touch your friend's toes with your toes."

Thanks to Jackie Hersh for the suggestion of giving the challenges very softly, and also of having children "touch your fingers with your friend's fingers," and so on.

pass the shoe

Life Skills	• Increasing attention span and concentration
	• Developing temporal awareness (timing)
	• Listening skills, passing on the beat
	• Developing eye-hand coordination
	• Taking responsibility within the group
	• Self-control; learning to stay calm while waiting for one's turn to come
	• Solving problems of anticipation and readiness
	• Developing manual dexterity and object manipulation
	• Changing one's focus—from object passed to object coming
Materials	• Several easily handled objects for passing should be available; large, soft trash balls might be good (see "Making Equipment at Little or No Cost" page 160).
	• Drum (optional)
Directions	All players sit in a circle. Clap or beat on a drum in a slow, steady rhythm. On the beat each player pretends to place something in front of the player to the left. The child with the object actually passes it to the player on the left. Play continues. If and when you feel the children would like to attempt a greater challenge, ask them if they would like to add another object to be passed.
	Have the children pass one object, counting and passing the object on the fourth beat. Later add a clap on the fourth beat for any child who does not have the object. When the children can do this, have those who do not have an object slap the floor as if they did have one. Then if

© Addison-Wesley Publishing Company, Inc.

they are ready for a new challenge, have the children slap the floor in front of the person to their left on the passing beat.

Have the players sing the song below to the tune of "London Bridge Is Falling Down," and pass the object on each "you." Clapping on the passing beat might help at first. As children pass the object, the song could be sung slowly with strong emphasis on the "you," allowing children to be ready to complete the pass when the object arrives in front of them. Find a good progression for your group.

Pass the shoe from me to you, me to you, me to you;
Pass the shoe from me to you, and do just as I do!

Comments and Suggestions

- Players who can't sing can just say the words or hum.
- Mishaps will usually occur. Time and practice will bring about improvement. Encourage trying but avoid pressing for perfection.
- It is fun for the players to realize that they are improving as a group.
- You may want to challenge the group by saying something like "Let's see if we can get it all the way around the circle."
- After the group is familiar with this activity you might want to stress how a good pass, in which the object is placed right in front of the person to the left, is really helpful.
- As group size increases, so does the length of time each child is waiting for a turn. If you have a large group and you have a second adult helper you may want to consider dividing the class into two groups. This usually works best after the children are familiar with the activity. You may want to prepare the children for this by asking who is willing to play in the second group. You are the best judge as to whether your children are ready for this.
- Note the first modification on page 122.

Simplifications and Challenges

- As a variation of this activity, have pairs of children sit and face each other, forming two lines. Give one object to each pair. Have pairs pass the object back and forth between themselves. This increases participation and eliminates waiting for a turn. Children are able to see their success; visual cues can help reinforce auditory cues. Once pairs have mastered this variation, you may wish to have groups of four or more pass two objects clockwise.
- Have all players clap the rhythm as a bean bag is passed. Add more bags, one at a time, as the group can handle them. Old gloves can be filled with beans to make the bean bags.
- After the group is fairly proficient the tempo can be increased, which will happen naturally. If this makes the activity too confusing for some, you may want to slow it down by taking a strong lead in the song.

It was Sherry McBride's idea to pass the objects between pairs or in small groups.
Thanks to Julie Stiefel for the beanbag idea and to Pat Sullivan for the glove beanbag suggestion.
Thanks to Carol Lerner for the saying or humming suggestion.

© Addison-Wesley Publishing Company, Inc.

pop up

Life Skills	• Focusing attention and concentration
	• Separating two things
	• Practicing careful sound differentiation
	• Learning to distinguish between different sound patterns
	• Decoding and interpreting information and making decisions as rapidly as possible
	• Getting the idea
	• Making decisions
	• Developing memory skills
Materials	• Pictures of animals, colors, numbers (optional)
Directions	Each child is either a bear or a bunny. Children stand up quickly when their team name is called. Children who are not called remain sitting. Players learn to pay attention but respond only to specific signals. Note the first variation in Simplifications and Challenges.
Comments and Suggestions	• This game can be played in limited space.
	• Children need lots of repetition and turns in order to learn, so you may want to start with only two categories.
	• "Getting the idea" may take some trial and error by the children, but this is also part of the process. Many teachers are unaware of how empowering discovering something for yourself really is for the young child. Most children will usually learn with time and trials. Try to be patient. It may be well worth the wait if this helps empower children.

Observe individual children's progress. If some children do not learn over time, try to determine why before simply correcting them. Your group may not be ready for this type of complex decoding and interpretation processing, or perhaps they need more specific preparation. If you can determine children's needs you may be able to offer game experiences to facilitate their growth, allowing them a sense of competency that would not otherwise be experienced.

- It might be helpful to have each child initially hold a picture of an animal, a color, or a number card. It may depend on your objective for playing the activity.

Simplifications and Challenges

- Hold up a picture of an animal, color, or number. Have the group name it. Be sure that children are familiar with the names of the pictures. You may want to divide the group in half, putting one half clearly to the left and the other clearly to the right. Explain that one group is, for example, "red," and the other is "green." Each group stands only when their group's color is held up or called. Try some red and green calls. You may want to use words only. Encourage children to help each other to "get the idea." This is much more empowering than if the answers come from you. Now tell children that you may try to trick them; they seem to love this kind of challenge. Call some other color. Pause and see what happens. Again, try to let the children figure it out. As you feel they are able to handle more, ask them if they think they are ready for an even bigger challenge. You might move to assigning teams words with the same initial consonant, like *two* and *ten*, *bears* and *bunnies*, *crows* and *cranes*.
- If your children are not ready for practice in careful sound differentiation you might say "I like to eat carrots" (bunnies stand), "I like to hop" (bunnies stand), "I like honey" (bears stand), and so on.
- Change the calls to stress other sound discriminations, such as words that begin with /sh/ and /ch/, /p/ and /b/, and so on.

rhythm sticks and rhythmic hand patterns

Life Skills
- Increasing focus, attention span, and concentration
- Patterning (recognition and duplication)
- Listening
- Thinking and decision making
- Coping with stress in a safe environment
- Persevering to improve or get the idea
- Practicing self-evaluation
- Developing temporal and physical coordination
- Practicing rhythm
- Developing unity with a group

Materials
- For rhythm sticks, see "Making Equipment at Little or No Cost," page 163.

Directions   Each participant has one or two rhythm sticks, roughly eight to twelve inches long and approximately an inch to an inch and a half in diameter (easily held in the player's hands). The sticks can readily be made by rolling newspaper to selected size, or the children can work without sticks. The players sit in a circle. A rhythm with a simple movement pattern is established. Example: Simply have the group tap to music and reach high over their heads when the music stops. Movement patterns should fit the level of the group and allow for some sense of challenge. Try different patterns and perhaps create progressive challenges over time.

- The activity can be done without sticks ("Rhythmic Hand Patterns").
- Children seem to like noise makers, perhaps because they can hear the effect they (the children) are having.
- Newsprint does tend to come off on the hands.
- Some leaders use wooden dowel rods for the rhythm sticks. Our experience has been that paper rhythm sticks are quieter, safer, easier to come by, and more apt to be reproduced at home by the children (perhaps with parental assistance).
- This is an activity that can be developed over several sessions.
- With some groups the hand pattern may pose a real challenge by itself. The game "Follow Me," without sticks, may be a good way to introduce "Rhythm Sticks."
- "Follow Me," "Can You?", and "Mirroring" could all lead up to this activity.
- Start by teaching "Follow Me." Then place the sticks in front of each child and say, "Follow Me." Do some preliminary motions without the sticks. Then pick up the sticks and set them back down—as a part of "Follow Me." At the end of the activity, lay the sticks on the floor in front of you and fold your arms in your lap. Have the children follow this same pattern and then gather up the sticks.
- Repetition of the pattern later may challenge children and also allow them to recognize their improvement.
- You may want to start very simply and then add a new motion as you feel the children are ready. This process is referred to as an "additive" approach to progression building.
- You may find that creating hand patterns (that the players do as a group) is an activity in its own right.

- When the children are familiar with this activity, it can be used as a pleasant attention-getting device. Simply start a rhythm and allow the children to join in as they become aware that the activity has begun. This might also be used to bring the group together for other activities. Perhaps it could be used to gather the children to return to the room from outside.

Simplifications and Challenges

- Challenge young children with a "Follow Me" type activity in which you slap your thighs, then clap your hands, then raise one hand and say, "1" and then raise the other hand and say, "1" again. Go on to 2, 3, 4, and so on. This allows children to be challenged at a variety of levels, while allowing time for mental processing. Because of their total involvement, the children also practice focusing, paying attention, and concentrating over an extended period of time.
- Some teachers have suggested that establishing a patterned routine to a favorite nursery rhyme or song is fun. They feel that children enjoy the satisfaction of knowing what comes next.
- Children can perform routines to special holiday tunes. These might then be presented at assemblies or for parents.
- As the children progress you might have them attempt to reach across their body and touch the opposite shoulder. This allows children to practice crossing the midline of their bodies.
- Allow children to try to march to a marching rhythm.
- This activity could be started in a circle as a rhythmic hand pattern game.

Thanks to Sharon Borish for the suggestion of having children tap to music and reach high when the music stops.
Mary Felix made the suggestion of playing "Follow Me," first without the sticks and then with them, to introduce this activity.
The counting pattern was suggested by Becky Boone.

rise and shine ^(H)

Life Skills
- Practicing control of emotional extremes
- Relaxing
- Developing spatial awareness (an awareness of space, relative distance, and relationships within space)
- Making decisions

Materials
- Something that rings, like an alarm clock (optional) would be helpful

Directions

The players pretend to be asleep. Move among them and test how relaxed they really are. (See first modification under Simplifications and Challenges.) At the sound of an alarm, they jump up and move quickly to another place, where they pretend to fall asleep again. (You might again test their relaxation.)

Comments and Suggestions
- The ability to relax quickly and for whatever time is available is a valuable skill and should be developed.
- Residual stress and tension can reduce a child's adaptability, increase irritability, and lead to difficult behavior.
- The ability to relax can be improved through practice.
- Also see "Letting Go."
- Have disabled children move as much as possible at the sound of the alarm.

Simplifications and Challenges

- While the players lie on the floor or sit in chairs, ask them to tense a particular body part (fist, face, shoulders) and then stretch out the tension, trying to feel the difference between the two. Move among the children and tell them you would like them to show you how relaxed they can be. Picking up a hand or arm, see if it can be freely moved. Return it gently to place. The child should neither assist you nor resist you. Remember that it takes time and practice to learn to relax.

- Have children pretend that they are turtles with their heads deep in their shells (shoulders up and chins down). Slowly they stretch out their long necks as far as they can reach and peer around. When the fox comes, they quickly pull back into their shells.

Thanks to Sherry McBride for the "turtle" variation.

robot

Life Skills	• Developing an awareness of space
	• Listening, analyzing, and following verbal directions
	• Translating verbal directions into accurate action
	• Developing motor planning, estimating distances
	• Generating alternative solutions
	• Developing leadership abilities; accepting responsibility for another
	• Formulating effective verbal statements for specific directions
	• Making decisions
	• Practicing self-evaluation

Materials   No special materials are needed.

Directions   All players have partners. One partner (the Commander) tells the other partner (the robot) how to move in specific ways (*forward, backward, left, right, stop, go,* and so on), so that the robot can progress around obstacles and on to a preset goal.

Comments and Suggestion
• Beginning with a demonstration using only a few robot pairs may result in less confusion until the players become more proficient.
• Having the robots walk with stiff knees seems to slow down the speed.

Simplifications and Challenges
• Introduce the game by being the Commander yourself and have the children be the robots. Discuss what a robot is and what it may be able to do. Decide on two or three simple commands and moves, such as *forward, backward, stop, go*. This will help to alleviate possible confusion and frustration.

roll it

Life Skills
- Practicing visual tracking (being able to follow the movement of the ball)
- Practicing visual figure and ground discrimination (the ability to separate the relevant from the irrelevant in a visual field)
- Developing temporal awareness (judging the rolling speed of a ball)
- Developing spatial awareness (estimation and relationships in space)
- Practicing body and space relationships
- Increasing attention span and concentration; refocusing as a ball changes direction or as more than one ball is rolling
- Handling stress (when more than one ball is introduced)
- Persevering
- Practicing self-control (not chasing the ball when it rolls out of play; rolling instead of throwing)

Materials
- Balls—eventually children will use one for every two or three players— or possibly bean bags or objects that slide for children who have difficulty controlling rolling balls or who dive to get a ball

Directions

Have the players sit in a tight circle on the floor with their legs spread out and their feet touching. Be sure to make allowances for any child who seems uncomfortable sitting this way. Roll out one ball and ask the children to catch it and then roll it to someone else. When children seem able to do this, gradually roll out more balls. The object of the activity is for the players to keep as many balls as possible rolling while still maintaining control.

Comments and Suggestions

- Ask the group if they can keep the ball moving and *on the ground.* When the group seems ready you might ask them if they feel they could handle two balls rolling at once. Gradually adding additional balls will allow you to determine the level of control the group can handle and to add or withdraw a ball accordingly.

- It might be a good idea to announce at the beginning that the children are not to go after a ball rolled out of the circle. If a child leaves the circle to retrieve a ball other balls will tend to roll through the space. Another possibility would be to establish the number of balls that can roll out (perhaps three) before the action is stopped to collect them. At some point you may want to bring it to the children's attention that the longer the balls stay in the circle the longer they can play without stopping.

- Since you may eventually want several balls, you might call your tennis-playing friends or local tennis club to collect old tennis balls.

- "Roll It" balls do not have to bounce or be "alive."

- Other types of balls can be used. Evaluate each for "safety" and success rate.

- Loss of equipment is frequently a problem in all play, but having sufficient balls for this game is important. At the end of the game, ask participants to help you find all the balls and toss them into the bag, perhaps having the group count each one as it goes into the bag. This is a simple trick that really works.

- When using bean bags on carpet you may need to put them in sandwich bags so that they will slide.

- When children kneel rather than sit, less space is needed but diving for a ball or bean bag is more apt to occur. You may want to indicate that an object should not be touched by a particular player until it touches his or her leg. If your children have difficulty with this it may be better to start with bean bags.

132

© Addison-Wesley Publishing Company, Inc.

Simplifications and Challenges

- If your group gets too excited when a ball is rolled back and forth, you may want to find an object that will slide rather than roll. This slows the pace of the activity and may help children maintain better self-control. Try to move to balls as soon as the children can handle them, since balls allow for more turns and less waiting. It is easier for children to share if they feel they will be getting lots of turns.
- Place an empty plastic liter soda bottle or gallon milk jug in the center of the circle for children to try to hit with the ball. If the activity becomes too rambunctious, a bottle partially filled with sand or dirt will be more stable.

Thanks to Brenda Hanthorne for the suggestion of telling children at the beginning of the game not to go after a ball that rolls out of the circle.

sounds to move by [(H)]

Life Skills
- Developing memory skills
- Using translation and decoding processes
- Practicing self-evaluation

Materials
- Sound makers (optional)

Directions

Large movements in place—such as hopping on one foot, running in place, jumping with two feet, making large backward arm circles, rotating head (both directions), circling hips (both directions)—are matched to specific sounds, such as clapping, finger snapping, clicking tongue, slapping thighs, beeping, honking, musical instruments, and so on.

When the players hear or see a given sound, they try to respond with the corresponding movement. For example, if the sound of a bell has been matched with running in place, then the players would run in place as the bell is rung. When the bell stops, the players stop; when the next sound is heard the players move according to the matched movement.

Comments and Suggestions
- The younger or more inexperienced the group, the fewer sounds should be used to start this game. Two or three may be sufficient. Let the children and their abilities grow gradually.
- Add another sound only as the children seem ready to accept the challenge. You may want to ask them if they think they are ready to add another sound.
- If the environment is conducive to allowing players to choose within their ability levels and leaders can create a broad range of challenges

to choose from, players will tend to progressively seek growth and challenge. When a participant is inattentive or out of control, factors beyond the immediate situation may be the cause, or the situation may be threatening (beyond a player's level of ability) or not sufficiently challenging.

- Checking your group two days later may give you evidence of the group's long-term memory development.

Simplifications and Challenges

- After the players have learned the basic format of the activity and have begun to be familiar with which sound corresponds to what movement, you might add another challenge by asking them if they can try to close their eyes whenever possible, relying only on hearing. At first some players will need to keep their eyes open all or part of the time, but try to observe these players over several sessions to see their progress. Allow each child to decide when she or he is ready for this challenge.
- "Trying to Remember" substitutes numbers for sounds.

squirrels in the trees

Life Skills
- Developing body and space relationships
- Developing motor planning
- Developing an awareness of the moving speed of another
- Practicing body control (balance, stopping and starting)
- Developing listening skills
- Practicing emotional and physical self-control when excited
- Showing consideration for and cooperation with others
- Making rapid decisions and adapting them if necessary
- Developing patience; waiting for a turn
- Developing agility, ability to stop and start quickly, change directions
- Solving problems
- Practicing self-control

Materials
- Butcher paper, paper grocery bags, or plastic hoops

Directions

Spread out several pieces of butcher paper. Tell the children that they need to walk and step onto the paper (tree) with some care in order to not slip or tear the tree. Have all the children stand on the available trees or have a tree for each child. A call of "acorns" sends squirrels gathering imaginary nuts (thus moving about in the space available). A call of "winter" sends the "squirrels" scurrying for the shelter of the trees. In this version all the children are squirrels all the time.

For older preschoolers, divide the group into threes. Any leftover participant will be an extra squirrel without a tree. We have found that even older young players do not like to be a tree for any length of time.

136

Our solution to this preference is to change roles with some regularity. Ask the three players to number off or to be a red, brown, or grey squirrel. Then practice having them remember their number or color by challenging them to raise their hands when their number or color is called. Call the numbers or colors out several times. During the game, ask various numbers or colors to step into the trees and be the squirrel.

In each group of three, two players join hands and form a tree for the third participant (the squirrel), who will stand between them. The leader calls, "Squirrels change trees." At this call, all trees raise their arms while the squirrels, including any extras, scramble to find a new tree. If there are extra squirrels, the challenge is to get to a free tree. If the group is even, the challenge is to change trees as quickly as possible. Young players seem to enjoy the excitement of the process itself; their idea of winning may be simply doing the activity.

Comments and Suggestions

- You may help children get the idea of the game by minimizing the initial structure. Use only one squirrel to demonstrate how the squirrel moves from tree to tree. Then gradually add additional squirrels until all are playing. Begin to eliminate trees (as in the game of "Islands") until all the squirrels are sharing a few trees.
- You may want to challenge the squirrels to try to find a different tree each time. Remember that this gets more difficult with each change.
- In the players-as-trees version in which a squirrel is not allowed to go back to any tree already occupied it is possible to begin to encourage a squirrel-to-squirrel helping relationship. When a player cannot find an unoccupied tree that he or she has not already gone to as a squirrel, then the leader can ask, "Can anyone help this squirrel to find a tree?" It may take a little time for the players to decide how to do this, but at least one player usually comes to this squirrel's rescue and then this behavior becomes a model for helping in this game and

other situations. Usually younger children offer to share their tree (fine solution), while older children suggest a switching solution.

- It may be important that the children have played "Cross Over," and are capable of handling their bodies in a crowd.
- If your group is very small or really needs to move more you may want to consider playing "Find It."
- Players who enjoy this game might also like "Busy Bee and Back to Back."
- Should there be only one squirrel to a tree? This may depend on group, the situation, or how many trees you want to have. The decision is yours.
- After children know this game it could also be played outside.

Simplifications and Challenges

- Near Halloween change "Squirrels in the Trees" to "Ghost in a Haunted Mansion" and signal a change of mansions by saying, "All ghosts come out." The ghosts all run to a new home while they are making a "Wooo Wooo" sound. They stop the sound when they have found a new home. With older children, start the game with groups of three in which one child is the ghost, one is a door, and the third is a window. This makes it easier for them to remember when changing positions. In this version the children who are the mansions (doors and windows) make the "Wooo Wooo" sound until their mansion is filled. This helps the ghosts who are left to find an available mansion.

Thanks to George Welsh for the variation in which all the children are squirrels all the time.
It was Sherry McBride's idea to use "acorns" and "winter" as movement signals.
Lori Romano suggested using only one squirrel when the game is first being introduced.
The Halloween variation was suggested by Marie Delfin.

streamers^(H)

Life Skills	• Developing body and space relationships • Generating ideas • Making something that can be shared with others • Cooperating, moving in unison, belonging and being responsible to a group, following, making contributions, sharing ideas, compromising, leading • Developing memory skills
Materials	• One crepe paper streamer for each participant • Music source (optional)
Directions	The players merely move a crepe paper streamer or cloth scarf around in the air in as many different circular patterns as possible. This is a simple but creative piece of play equipment that has been with us, in one form or another, since players first found pleasure in watching a ribbon, scarf, or piece of paper flutter through currents of air. For more information about making streamers, see page 165, "Making Equipment at Little or No Cost."
Comments and Suggestions	• This can be an opportunity for individual, quiet involvement; an opportunity to participate in a demonstration for others; a break on long car trips; or a present to make and share with a friend. • Perhaps your group would like to participate in a demonstration for parents or other groups. • This activity is possible for all skill levels and at the same time helps the participant develop physically, emotionally, and socially.

- The streamers can be used individually or in a group.
- Encourage the children to try to use both arms to move the streamers; the tendency is to use only the dominant side.
- You may want to start with big, slow motions in a "Follow Me" activity.
- Incorporate classical music into the activity. The tempo of the music may make a difference as to how peacefully or vigorously the children move the streamer.

Simplifications and Challenges

- The following could be played with streamers:

  "Follow Me"   "Mirroring"
  "Can You Do This?"   "Trying to Remember"
  "Cross Over"

- Perhaps a creative physical therapist could develop range-of-motion activities for players to do on their own between therapy sessions.
- Use the streamers in play-acting situations, such as roping calves, cracking whips, fly casting, and so on.

tiger, tiger, where's the tiger? (H)

Life Skills
- Focusing, attending
- Practicing listening skills and directional discrimination of sound
- Developing spatial awareness (an awareness of space, relative distance, and relationships within space)
- Making decisions
- Practicing self-evaluation

Materials
No special materials are needed.

Directions
Tell the children that you would like them to help you find the tiger. They are to close their eyes and listen very carefully. When they hear the tiger they are to point toward it. Move a short distance, stop, and roar like a tiger. Ask the children to open their eyes to see if they were able to find the tiger while their eyes were closed. Repeat several times. Roar loudly sometimes and more softly sometimes. Ask for a volunteer to help you by being a tiger. All other players close their eyes. The tiger moves around the room with you. Stop and signal the tiger to roar. Then say to the group, "Tiger, tiger, where's the tiger?" All players with eyes closed point toward the tiger and say, "Tiger, tiger, there's the tiger!" The children then open their eyes and evaluate their accuracy. Let various children volunteer to be the tiger. As the children begin to catch on you may want to attempt to let the tiger roam alone and then signal it to roar.

Comments and Suggestions

- Having the leader be the first tiger for a period of time allows the children to get the idea.
- Tigers sometimes forget that they are to stop before they roar. You may want to have a stop signal or call, "Tiger freeze," so that you can stop the moving tiger before indicating that it should roar.
- This might be a good opportunity to assess hearing ability.
- Do not worry about peeking. As the children get used to the game they will peek less. Remember that they are naturally curious.
- Before asking for a volunteer to be a tiger, allow the entire group to audition for the role of tiger. Have all the players roar at once (this always seems to let off a bit of steam).
- Be aware that children will need enough space to point without accidentally poking another while their eyes are closed.

Simplifications and Challenges

- If you are in a place where excessive noise is going to be a problem, you might like to modify this game to "Kitty, kitty, where's the kitty?" This also increases the challenge.
- Have the children close their eyes and try to follow a variety of sounds: snapping fingers, clapping hands, jingling keys, and so on. Periodically stop and say, "Check," to let the children open their eyes to evaluate their aim. Then say, "Close," and go on.

142

trying to remember

Life Skills	• Increasing attention span and concentration • Developing recall • Releasing tension and excessive energy • Accepting a challenge • Practicing self-evaluation
Materials	No special materials are needed.
Directions	Select or have the players select movements (such as clapping hands, running in place, alternate reaching of hands overhead as high as possible, head circles, hip rotations) and assign a number to each action. The object is to try to remember what number calls for what movement.
Comments and Suggestions	• Begin with a few movements and add to them as the group is ready. • Encourage participants to avoid outside clues whenever possible. To encourage this, emphasize trying rather than being right. • You may want to alternate very active movements with less active movements to allow for recovery.
Simplifications and Challenges	• List several baseball actions and give each a number: 1 = pitching, 2 = batting; 3 = running, 4 = umpire signaling "out" and 5 = umpire signaling "safe." Have the group do the appropriate motion as you call each number. • Another technique used is to challenge the players to close their eyes.

Thanks to Gloria Grisham for the baseball variation.

weather walks^(H)

Life Skills
- Generating alternatives
- Developing individual interpretations
- Expressing oneself
- Developing spatial awareness (an awareness of space, relative distance, and relationships within space)
- Developing creativity and individual decision making
- Developing environmental awareness
- Using the body as a means of expression

Materials

No special materials are needed.

Directions

Have players dramatize all forms of weather by walking as if they were feeling it.

Comments and Suggestions

- Possible weather conditions:

windy	fall, walking in leaves	sunny
hurricane	puddles after a rain	tornado
very hot	lightning storm	very cold
drizzle	icy	humid; very little breeze

- Weave a story around the weather.
- Stories can become more involving when a participant can imagine the feeling of a particular weather condition. Weather is frequently used to set a mood in a story.
- Perhaps you can have players do a daily weather report. This might start with a sunrise and end with a sunset:

© Addison-Wesley Publishing Company, Inc.

The sun will rise (children can choose movements that are slow and big) *at 5:23 AM this morning. The morning will be sunny* (children select a movement they feel is appropriate to show "sunny"), *with light showers* (movement to show "light showers" can be selected by each child) *expected this evening. Sunset will be at 8:44 PM* (each child selects movements).

End with a condition that is quiet to relax the group.

Simplifications and Challenges

- Have the players walk as if they are in various substances or places:

in deep snow	on eggs	in oil
around a sleeping tiger	in deep sand	on ice
in molasses or glue	on a tightrope	in puddles
on hot coals or hot sand		

- Have the players walk as if they were in certain places:

through a toy shop	at a circus	in a zoo
through a dream	in a jungle	in a dark house
through a jar of jam	in a park	on a busy street
in a house with a million friendly cats		

- The players could do mood walks (sad, happy, tired, worried, and so on).
- They could walk like a bear, a centipede, a baby just learning to walk, a toad, a kangaroo, an inchworm, and so on.
- Use music such as "The Grand Canyon Suite" to set the pace.
- Ask the players for other possibilities and also let yourself be creative.
- A challenge might be to do the movement in slow motion.

Sharon Harrison suggested using music to set a walking pace.

what is different? (H)

© Addison-Wesley Publishing Company, Inc.

Life Skills
- Practicing visual alertness and pattern recognition
- Developing visual sensitivity to change
- Monitoring the details of one's environment; noticing change and responding appropriately
- Developing short-term memory skills
- Practicing self-evaluation

Materials

No special materials are needed.

Directions

Challenge the players to look carefully at everything about you. Then ask them to close their eyes. Change one thing about your appearance. Ask them to open their eyes, but caution them not to tell if they see what it is. Then ask a series of questions to give those who do not notice the difference a chance to succeed in finding the secret (what is different). Ask, "How many think the change is above my waist? Below my waist? Below my knees? Above my shoulders? Something about my clothing? At the count of three, point to what is different." Repeat the activity.

Comments and Suggestions
- Start with a very obvious change to allow the children to get the idea.
- Make the challenges more difficult as children are able to handle them.
- As the children get the idea and are comfortable with the activity, ask for a volunteer to be the leader. Do not ask for volunteers too soon, or only those who catch on quickly will volunteer to lead.
- Two participants can play this game.
- Children could play this game at home with their parents.

where is...?(H)

Life Skills
- Developing a sense of location and orientation in relation to local surroundings
- Listening
- Dealing with excitement and suspense
- Practicing mental processing and decision making
- Practicing self-evaluation with an opportunity to sense improvement

Materials

No special materials are needed.

Directions

The leader calls out a challenge clue for a specific direction ("Where are the windows?" "Where are the blocks?"). The players try to face in that direction.

Comments and Suggestions
- Since each participant receives immediate feedback, it is usually not necessary to correct errors. If players are allowed to correct their own errors immediately, more fun and challenge may occur.
- If you would like to increase the suspense and sense of challenge, simply pause before you say the final word.
- If you wish to increase the sense of challenge even more, simply say the final word in a somewhat quick and excited manner after the above-mentioned pause.
- Remember, in activities that require cognitive processing, it is important to give sufficient processing time AFTER you give the clue to allow all players an opportunity to learn from the experience.
- The points of orientation are limitless. Have fun with these. What

would be valuable for your preschoolers to know?

- Knowing where places and things are tends to make people more comfortable.
- It might be helpful to have the players talk about why knowing where things are is important.
- This activity may help children become more alert to where things are around them.

Simplifications and Challenges

- Vary places and locations.
- Add aspects of physical fitness to the activity. ("Where are the blocks? Turn toward them and run in place.")
- When outside you may do "Magic Circling." Ask the children "Where is...?" and ask them to encircle it.
- Put words or colors or pictures of animals on the walls and use them as clues to play the game.

where is it? (H)

Life Skills	• Listening; determining the direction from which a sound comes • Developing an awareness of space • Practicing self-control • Practicing self-evaluation
Materials	• Keys or something that will make a sound
Directions	The children stand in a circle. They put their hands behind their backs and close their eyes. The leader walks around the circle behind the players, rattling an object. Stopping behind one player, the leader shakes the object vigorously and then places it in the hand of the player. Then the leader moves away from that player and calls for eyes to be opened. On the count of three, all the players are to point to the child they believe has the object. The object is then revealed and the game continues.
Comments and Suggestions	• After children learn this game they can volunteer to be the leader. • If you select leaders other than the children who have been the receivers of the noise maker you can double the number of children chosen, and also prevent a child from never being chosen. • You might also ask for a helper who remembers who hasn't had a turn yet to be a leader or a receiver of the noisemaker.
Simplifications and Challenges	• Have two leaders circulate with two objects to pinpoint. • Create more than one group. • Have children pass the object behind their backs. When you signal them to stop, they identify the child holding the object.

wind, rain, and thunder (H)

Life Skills
- Being a contributing part of an effectively functioning group
- Focusing attention and concentration over time
- Bonding
- Getting the idea; putting factors together (discovery) without adult evaluative intervention

Materials   No special materials are needed.

Directions   Have children sit in a circle or in seats. Ask each player to duplicate whatever you are doing. Rub your hands together (wind). Then begin patting your thighs or tapping the floor (rain). Then begin stomping your feet (thunder). Build from the quiet sound of the wind into the sound of rain and then into thunder. Continue to challenge the group by shifting between these three motions. End the activity by reversing the original sequence, which allows for a calming from the storm. Perhaps the final motions could be the folding of hands, asking the children to close their eyes and try to imagine a rainbow. After a period of quiet, you might have the children awake and pat themselves on the back for a job well done.

Comments and Suggestions
- The activity can end with a very peaceful feeling.
- The activity can have an almost magical unifying effect on the group.

Simplifications and Challenges

- A year-long challenge might be "One Behind," in which the children begin the motion that you have been doing as you move on to the next.

Thanks to Steve Moyer for introducing us to "Wind, Rain, and Thunder."

the winds are changing

Life Skills
- Bonding
- Making decisions
- Becoming more aware of one's similarities and differences in relation to others.
- Developing spatial awareness (an awareness of space, relative distance, and relationships within space)
- Getting the idea; putting factors together (discovery) without adult evaluative intervention

Materials   No special materials are needed.

Directions   Players sit (or stand) in a circle. A series of questions are asked. Those answering "yes" move to the opposite side of the circle.

Present sets of questions that enable all children to move. Examples of questions:

Do you have a sister? Do you have a brother? Are you the only child in your family?

Are you wearing sneakers today? Are you wearing something other than sneakers today?

Are you wearing blue? (Include other colors.)

Be sure everyone gets a chance to move.

Comments and Suggestions

- This activity can allow a child to practice making decisions. This struggle may make later decision making easier. Because this process may involve a period of fumbling in the decision-making process, adults may feel they need to speed up the process by helping a child to find the answer. While at times this may be necessary, be aware that this could reduce that child's opportunity to experience the decision-making process. Our task is to try to engineer the environment so that the child can experience this process.
- Make up questions to fit your group. This may give you and your group more awareness of each other and may allow some children an additional sense of comfort and belonging.
- Asking questions with yes or no answers can guarantee that all have an opportunity to move.
- Use this activity as a lead-in to "Cross Over."

Simplifications and Challenges

- Have players use carpet skates on their feet.
- Have children hop, skip, or slide across the circle.
- Have younger children stand in two lines.
- Present children with two choices. Players must choose one of the two and move to the place specified for each choice. Examples of pairs of choices:

  Would you rather eat a peanut butter sandwich or an apple?

  Would you rather paint a picture or hear a story?

  Would you rather sing a song or build with blocks?

making equipment at little or no cost

Making equipment is both fun and easy, and there are many advantages to having players participate in this process. Since the materials are frequently things thrown away, the players normally have access to them, and their use may prove to be beneficial.

There is a sense of competency and pride that comes in making something yourself. If players can see the produced object as something they created themselves, they will be more likely to use it, thereby increasing eye-hand coordination, throwing ability, and other perceptual skills.

Players can also create gifts for younger brothers and sisters and experience giving and sharing. Equipment can be made to the size, softness, and weight that fits individual users. This is not always possible with mass-produced, standardized equipment. Many handmade pieces of equipment are safer than commercially mass-produced equipment. Items made of paper, yarn, and cloth are generally softer and safer for group play.

Another advantage of handmade equipment is that repairs and replacements are easy and immediate. A quick trip to the basement starts the whole creative or re-creative process. Thinking up new ideas may allow for initiative and problem solving. It may also stimulate the creative process.

Encourage players to help by making their own equipment. This also increases the possibilities of their making additional equipment for use at home or with friends.

Making a piece of junk equipment that children play with over and over extends the hours of connectedness between parent and child. This piece of junk equipment also sparks a memory each time it is played with.

balls

Yarn balls

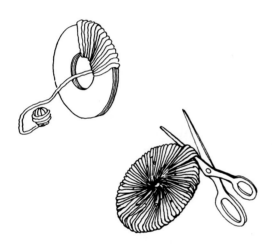

The first approach, in which the yarn is wrapped around cardboard donuts, will take about five times longer than the second approach (Floppy, Quick-to-Make Yarn ball), in which the yarn is wrapped around a VHS box with the cassette in it. However, the cardboard donut approach usually produces a ball that is rounder, firmer (although it should still be soft), and more apt to roll. The ball made from recycled yarn mentioned in the second approach seems to have the advantages of roundness, softness, roll, and requires less time to make. The VHS floppy yarn ball has advantages in its floppiness. It is easier to catch and to retrieve. Each ball will have its own uniqueness based upon type and amount of yarn used and approach selected.

Donut yarn balls

You will need:
- scrap yarn
- cardboard
- fishing line or strong string

From two approximately 7-inch-square pieces of cardboard cut two donut-shaped patterns. The inside hole should be roughly 3 inches in diameter. Place the two donuts together and begin wrapping the yarn through the donut hole until the center hole is nearly filled. Since you will have to use smaller and smaller balls of scrap yarn to pass through

157

the narrowing center hole, you will have to knot the yarn frequently. The knots are no problem if they are tied securely.

Cut down between the two pieces of cardboard. Separate the pieces slightly and tie the yarn between them with strong line or string. Tie as tightly as possible and secure the string or line with at least a double knot. A second tie might be wise. Gently pull the cardboard off over the yarn. Fluff the yarn and trim it if it is not quite round.

Floppy, quick-to-make yarn balls

You will need
- heavy scrap yarn (about 2 skeins)
- fishing line or strong string
- scissors
- VHS video cassette or box with cassette in it

Wrap the yarn around the length of the VHS cassette. Wrapping the yarn around the width of the box will make a smaller ball. When the yarn seems very thick, carefully slide the yarn off the box. Tie the yarn in the middle. You may want to use two separate pieces of triple yarn for strength if you don't have strong string or fishing line. Pull these ties as tight as possible to help hold the yarn ball together. Cut the top and bottom "loops" of yarn. If you are using scissors, it may help to have someone hold the yarn while you cut. Shake the ball and trim stray ends if you wish. Don't worry if your creation is not quite round. Using yarn that has been recycled from a knitted or crocheted garment will make a wonderful curly ball.

Comments
- Heavy yarn or rug yarn wraps more quickly and makes good yarn balls, although these will not have as much body as balls made with regular yarn.
- Many people who knit have extra ends of scrap yarn. Usually they are more than glad to donate the yarn.

158

- Making a yarn ball requires time and patience. You may want to seek volunteers to help.
- Save any scraps, trimmings, or pieces of yarn to make into a small ball. Tie off the toe of a stocking at a level that avoids any runs or weaknesses. Turn the stocking inside out, so that the knot is inside. Fill the stocking with these scraps of yarn until it is the shape of a ball. Tightly tie off the open end. Trim off any excess.
- You can purchase commercially made fleece or yarn balls from school equipment catalogs if you have more money than patience. Soft balls are very good pieces of equipment if you must work in a small space or room used for other purposes. Two other forms of balls that can be made to supplement the yarn balls or be used instead of yarn balls are sock and trash balls.

Sock balls

You will need
- old socks or a single sock
- newspaper or any stuffing material
- rubber bands or needle and thread (optional)

You can use two socks and roll and tuck as some do for storing clean socks. Or you can stuff a single sock with soft materials, such as newspaper. Tuck in the excess material. Place rubber bands around the sock to hold it together, or stitch it closed.

Trash balls

- newspaper
- tape or rubber bands
- some old plastic bags

Wad the newspaper into a ball shape, cover it with a plastic bag, and tape or secure it with rubber bands.

Warning: Plastic bags can be dangerous. It is recommended that you punch holes in all plastic bags prior to their use.

Suggestions
- Do not feel limited to round balls. Some not-so-perfectly-round balls can add a challenge.
- Soccer balls will need to be made a little more durable but are good for indoor practice and play.
- Plastic foam sheets used in packing materials are an excellent substitute for the newspaper.

carpet skates

Pieces of carpet cut to an inch or two longer than the child's foot and a little wider than the foot can be placed under each foot, reducing the amount of speed that can be built up and making it possible for children to be active in less space. Carpet skates may also provide a vigorous workout of the abdominal muscles and the legs and can in some situations even provide a cardiovascular workout.

If floors are carpeted, make the skates out of cardboard, shoe boxes, or shoe box lids. Be sure that the surface of the skate that will be placed against the carpet does not have print or colors on it that can leave marks on the carpet.

sticks, bats, and rackets

Racket

You will need

- strong wire coat hanger
- one nylon stocking or leg of panty hose
- masking tape
- scissors
- about six feet of thin ribbon or yarn
- a balloon
- a pair of pliers to shape the handle of the racket

Bend the coat hanger into a rectangular or square shape. Straighten or bend the hook of the hanger to form a handle. This may require a pair of pliers. Pull the foot of the stocking over the top of the hanger and work down toward the handle. Pull tight so that a bouncy surface is formed. Wrap the stocking around the handle to give some protection to the hand, and tape it in place. Cut off any bulky excess.

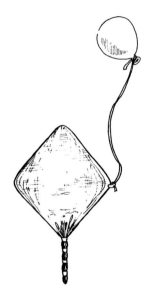

If you wish to attach a balloon to the racket for an individual game, blow a balloon up about three quarters of its normal size so that there will be less chance of it breaking, and tie it off securely. Fasten the ribbon or yarn to the balloon and to the racket at the handle, or make a small hole at one corner of the racket face and tie the yarn to the racket. Use a shorter length of ribbon for younger children. Some children will choose to remove the ribbon for greater challenge, or find a friend with whom to hit the balloon back and forth.

These rackets are fun and can be given as gifts.

Newspaper bat

You will need
- newspaper
- tape

Tightly roll sheets of newspaper to make a bat. It helps if you develop a rolling technique that finishes with a fold rather than with many edges on the outside. Secure the roll with tape.

162

Rhythm sticks

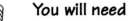

You will need
- newspaper
- tape
- plastic bags (optional)

To make rhythm sticks, follow the directions above for the newspaper bat. Rhythm sticks are shorter, and can be made in various sizes, so you will want to fold your newspaper accordingly before rolling. If desired, cover the sticks with plastic bags; secure with tape.

scoop catchers

You will need
- Plastic gallon milk jugs

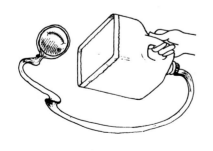

Notes: Rinse milk jugs thoroughly. If you immediately cut out the bottom you will have less "souring." Save caps.

Using a sharp knife or scissors, carefully cut the bottom out of the plastic jug. Tape the cut edges for safety. You now have a scoop catcher. Besides being a lot of fun, this scoop will encourage proper force absorption and a good follow-through.

Place a soft ball in the toe of a nylon stocking, and put the other end through the pour spout opening, and then fasten it by screwing the cap on to create a ball and scoop catcher that can be used by a solitary player.

plastic hoops

You will need

- Flexible PVC or drinking fountain tubing—100 inches for each standard-sized hoop
- a wooden dowel rod that fits snugly within the tubing, or the plastic connector sold with the tubing
- super glue or substitute
- vinyl plastic tape (optional)

Plumbing tubing comes in a variety of diameters, making it possible to create your own lifetime, durable plastic hoops that can be used for activities like "Islands."

The tube with a diameter about the size of a commercially-made plastic hoop can be warmed with a hair dryer or hot water and curved to form a circle. A standard hoop is approximately 100" around, but you can vary this size.

To complete the hoop, warm the cut ends of the hoop and attach them by inserting a plastic connector. An alternate method is to take a one-inch piece of wooden dowel that fits snugly inside the tubing, put an adequate amount of super glue on the rod, and use it to secure the two ends together, and let dry. If you wish to add color to your new plastic hoops you can add vinyl plastic tape, which comes in several colors.

streamers

You will need

- crepe paper (rolls or package)
- scissors
- cardboard (optional)
- tape, brads, staples (optional)

If you are using packaged crepe paper, cut strips approximately two to three inches wide. Make them long enough so that each child can successfully create a circular pattern as the streamer is moved through the air. You may want to attach the strips of crepe paper to a cardboard handle with tape, brads, or staples.

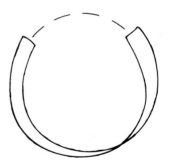